HALO ROBERTS

Finding My Night
A Boss/Assistant Romantic Comedy

Second edition

ISBN: 978-1-7770505-5-9

Cover art by Teshia Saunders
Advisor: Terri Stepek

This book was professionally typeset on Reedsy.
Find out more at reedsy.com

I can't thank that guy enough for giving me the time to do this, he's the best.

"A day without sunshine is like, you know, night."

-Steve Martin

Contents

I   Part 1: The Not-A-Date...Date

Oops	3
Caught Daydreaming	4
It Doesn't Feel Like Work	7
Be My Plus One?	10
Fancy...for Work	16
It's a Date...Right?	18
I Think This Might Be A Date	24
A Mansion in the Woods	29
The Cream Puff Fiasco	33
Time To Take a Chance	42
Better Than a Daydream	46
The Night is Still Young	48
Oh, My, Yes...	52
Yes. Mine.	54
Can't Stand the Heat?	57
She Was Here	62
The Beginning of 'Us'	67
Don't Piss Off a Rich Man	76
An Unexpected Visitor	82
Out of the Frying Pan	84
Damn, This is Perfect	88

Nick's Desk? Check. 91

This Will Hold Me Over 93

It's the Little Things 95

Mrs Henderson's Gift 98

Dinner in the Burbs 102

Party in the Burbs 106

Behind the Ink 111

What's in a Name? 114

The Surprise 117

Final Romp at the Loft 120

And Babies Make Four 122

II   Part 2: A Night Wedding

Margo's On the Job 127

Taming the Silver Fox 131

A Bumpy Beginning 134

Let's Try This Again 138

The Do-Over 141

Let the Games Begin 145

A Detour Down Memory Lane 148

Ohmygod I Did That 152

Play for a Dance 154

Oil and Water 159

Night Swimming 162

Shut Up and Kiss Me 167

Stop Thinking So Hard 169

Gosh 173

Hey Babe 176

Last Call 178

The Deal Breaker 183

Incubator Blues   185

Swing and a Miss   190

Oh…You…Gahhhh   192

I Saved This For You   195

Cheers   199

Moon and Stars   202

Hitched Without A Hitch   207

The Most Perfect Thing   210

You've Got Mail   212

Read on for a taste of the next story…it's

Veronica's, and…   214

Finding My One   215

Rude Awakening   216

Pause for Effect   218

Tough Love Sucks   220

About the Author   226

Also by Halo Roberts   228

I

Part 1: The Not-A-Date...Date

Oops

⁂

*S*lamming his hand down on the desk he snarls into the phone, "I can't believe you're going to miss this, it's the biggest opening I have this year and you'd rather be on some damn boat..." his voice trails off and he drops his forehead to his hand as he listens, anger and disappointment apparent in the hard set of his jaw and those full lips. Finally, after it seems like the voice on the line has talked forever, laughter comes through. I can barely hear it as I pause, not really even pretending to dust anymore. I watch his jaw flex as he growls, "Don't bother sweetheart, you're not worth it."

Dropping the dust cloth I cross the room, pull the phone out of his hands, and whisper into the speaker, "You don't deserve him." Disconnecting on an outraged female voice, I toss the phone to the side and quickly silence all of his questions by smashing my lips to his, first insistent, then softer...

Caught Daydreaming

Breanna

"**B**reanna…Breanna…Breanna!?"

Snapping out of my reverie, I startle to find dark eyes peering into mine. Holding the dust cloth in his hand, he carefully shakes my shoulder looking adorably annoyed. *Oh my fresh hell, did I seriously just daydream sex while he was on the phone five feet away. Did I say anything? Why did I actually drop the dust cloth, shit-shit-shit he is still looking at me, SAY SOMETHING BREE YOU FREAKING IDIOT.*

"Oh my goodness Mr. Mason, I am so sorry, I do *not* know where my head went." *I sound like a Southern belle, what the hell is wrong with me?* Carefully snatching the dust cloth out of his hand, trying not to visibly shiver at the heat of his skin as his fingers brush mine, I turn and attempt a graceful exit.

"I'll just finish in here later, I can see you're very busy, I'll just be in the kitchen," I've managed to stumble to the door as he looks at me with concern that is quickly fading as he becomes distracted by some papers on the table.

Picking them up and crossing back to his desk he mutters, "I've told you, Nick is fine." Without looking at me again he becomes engrossed in something on his computer.

"Sure Nick, as long as you'll call me Bree," I reply so softly I'm sure he doesn't hear. Carefully closing the door, I take my mortified self to the kitchen.

Leaning against the counter, fingers curled over the stainless steel edge, I let the cool metal calm me down. Daydreaming in the boss' home office while he is having an angry conversation with Veroni*bitch*. Not cool but salvageable. Lunch should go a long way towards glossing over my little faux pas, I shove off the counter and head for the huge double fridge.

Humming lightly to myself, I take stock and decide on grilled salmon, butternut squash in parmesan with brown butter and a good salad. As my hands prepare the fish for the grill and get butter melting in the saute pan for the squash, my mind wanders back to my boss.

Nicholas Mason, art dealer and notoriously reclusive bachelor, the tabloids that follow Veroni*bitch* say he's 38, somewhere over six feet tall with shoulders that say he works out for strength. His dark hair is always carefully pulled back at the nape of his neck but if he let it loose, *delicious shiver from bellybutton to hoo-ha*, it would brush his shoulders in black waves that match the beard he keeps carefully trimmed. His clothes are expensive and perfect. Everything about him is perfect, it makes me nervous, it sets him apart, sometimes he doesn't even seem human.

I've been secretly pining for the man for almost eight months now, but with Veronica in the picture, he wouldn't notice me if I cooked in a belly-dancer ensemble with a fruit basket on my head. I mean, seriously, he attends star-studded events with a socialite who is so loaded that she could become Empress of her own island if it took her fancy.

Me? I'm Breanna from the suburbs. Compared to Veronica? I'm nobody.

It Doesn't Feel Like Work

Breanna

I had just started working for Nick, getting used to the job, probably best described as maid/personal chef, in his loft apartment in the heart of downtown. I couldn't even imagine the rent, but if he could afford this, it made sense that he could afford having me come over every day to take care of the place. I fell into the job by chance, completely right place, right time.

I was in culinary school, close to finishing, but money was tight. Frank, one of the chefs in charge of my final course, was moonlighting catering intimate dinner parties for the high end art crowd. One evening, Nick happened to ask him if he knew anyone who would like to keep up the apartment and take care of his meals when he was home. His job demands a lot of travel and weird hours, so he was hoping to just hire privately and avoid all of the complications of a service. Frank, bless that man to the moon, recommended me, and after a background check and a five minute phone interview, I was given a trial. One week to make sure I was the right fit. Even though that was almost eight months ago, one of my favorite daydreams still centers on that first day.

Arriving at the loft, maybe 15 minutes earlier than arranged, I let myself in with the key I was given by Nick's business partner when I stopped at his office to sign the paperwork. A tall, cool-faced man with a long, regal nose and silver hair cut tight to his head, Sanford Williams, *you may call me Mr. Williams,* quickly outlined the job and handed me a key and a credit card so that I could keep the apartment stocked with food and other essentials.

As I came in the door, I heard music coming from the end of the hall. I recognized a few bars of an old song, the beat was heavy and the volume was loud. Smiling, I turned into the kitchen and passed through to the walk-in pantry to put away my purse and coat.

I walked back out to the kitchen, and there he was, his back to me, reaching into the fridge for a bottle of water that he cracked and gulped down to about half before turning. He jerked at the sight of me, sloshing a little water on his chest, but it was okay *because the man was only wearing a pair of black shorts.* Sweat glistening on his shoulders and little trickles running down through the curls of hair on his chest that narrowed into a delightful V disappearing into the band of the shorts, he made a funny noise between a gasp and a squawk before recovering.

I was busy trying not to stare at the beautiful ink swirling from his right pec around his rib cage and up over his shoulder. All black and shadows, his tats were done by someone who knew their shit; they were amazing, a blend of birds and gears and some words I couldn't make out because I realized I was gaping like a fish and jerked my gaze up to meet his eyes.

His surprise had been replaced by a small smile as I stared at him, and I blushed right to the roots of my blonde hair *damn pale skin.* He smoothly took in my dark jeans and fresh pressed white oxford.

"You must be Breanna, you're early." Not sure if I should apologize, I settled for a nod and looked around the kitchen as if I were interested in the equipment, which of course led me to wondering about his *equipment,* which led to a new round of blushing.

Before the silence could get weird, *too late*, I asked him some questions about routine, meal preferences and logistics, reminding myself that I can, in fact, be a professional. Nick seemed pleased and answered my questions thoughtfully before glancing at the clock.

"Well Breanna, it was nice to meet you," Nick said formally, his voice deep and smooth. "I hope this works out well for both of us. And now, I need to get ready, I have buyers to meet this afternoon."

"Dinner at seven?" I smiled brightly, he nodded and I watched his back, his ass, and that beautiful ink walk out of the kitchen.

Be My Plus One?

Breanna

*O*f course, in my daydreams, I am so much smoother. I say something witty, he proposes on the spot, we spend the rest of the day in bed, in the shower, in front of the fireplace and on his desk...

Quietly laughing at myself, I turn my attention back to lunch and wonder about the bit of phone call that I heard this morning. I've been arriving late morning to do a little cleaning and to prepare lunch if Nick is home. He often works from his home office, especially in the morning, so we've fallen into a pretty smooth routine. Unfortunately for me, he moved his workout to earlier in the morning, probably to avoid any more mostly naked encounters. *I have a good memory and an even better imagination, so I'm coping.*

I'm just assuming he was talking to Veronica, *Veronibitch,* especially with the comment about the boat. Veronica's daddy has enough money to fund several small countries and he regularly attempts to buy her love with things like boats and race horses and jewelry. Apparently her hobby became collecting art a few months ago, and that's how she and Nick became an item.

I haven't figured out what their exact status is, but if she stays overnight, she's gone well before I arrive, and there's ever only one coffee cup by the sink. Not a speck of her stuff in the entire apartment, no toothbrush in his bathroom, so all signs point to her not sleeping here and he does. *Which makes me so happy, I've nicknamed her Veronibitch for good reason.* I've only even seen her at the loft once, she came through like a whirlwind, angry that he was making her late to meet someone named "Mimsy" for drinks. My romantic little heart likes to believe that he's holding out for someone better, *me,* and that she is just interesting to him as a beautiful customer.

Then reality rears its stupid head and reminds me that I am domestic help, saving up to open a tiny restaurant. He is so far out of my league we aren't even playing the same sport.

Carefully putting together two plates of food, I leave them on the counter and walk halfway down the hall to his office and knock. When I hear his deep voice say, "Come", *shiver swoon,* I open the door.

"Would you like me to bring you lunch at your desk?"

Scruffing a hand through his beard and then unconsciously smoothing it back into place, he shakes his head.

"No, I'll eat in the kitchen, I need a break anyway." Standing and stretching his long arms above his head, *double swoon, so many ripples,* he leads the way.

Setting the plates at the table, we eat in comfortable silence.

11

The first few times I didn't eat, until he told me it was way too formal for me to just stand behind the counter waiting to see if he needed anything. After a short pause, he had wistfully added, "Also I'm an only child, my parents travelled constantly for my father's work. I always wished the nannies and housekeepers left with my care had wanted to just eat with me, like a family," in his deep, quiet voice.

For just a second there was a lost look in his eyes that I desperately wanted to kiss away, but I had chuckled as I thought of my own family.

"I wish I could have given you some of mine, being the oldest of five kids, I can't remember the last time I had a quiet meal," his eyes widened slightly and I heard a real honest laugh come straight from his belly. I joined him, and we have eaten together ever since.

"Is the gallery opening for a new talent?" We never talk a lot, but today, he is quiet in a more somber way, and I wonder again about the call with Veronica. Having zero idea how to broach the subject, and afraid I'd be way out of line, I decide it's safer to ask him about the gallery opening.

"Yes, actually," Nick's face lights up and his dark eyes meet mine. "It was rather remarkable luck, I decided to meet Williams at a restaurant I'd never been to before and just down the way, a man was painting the most incredible portraits." Pausing to take a bite, Nick's eyes are far away, remembering. "His name is James and he was using any bits of supplies he could find, spray paint, cardboard, bits of charcoal."

"What made you stop to look at his work?" Nick smiles at my question.

"He apologized and started to move the woman he was doing a portrait of out of the way, and I was able to see exactly how

keen his eye was for the details, the life he brings to his work…
it's really something." Nick shakes his head, pausing to take a
few more bites.

"It's so easy to assume that everyone on the street is on drugs
or drunk," he continues, "I don't know what made me stop
and talk to him, I guess I was just so intrigued by his art, but I
bought him a cup of coffee and asked him what brought him
to this place in life." Nick shrugs, glancing at me. "I felt kind
of bad after the words left my mouth, but James didn't seem
insulted at all… it was almost like he couldn't believe I would
want to know his story."

"I think we're all probably guilty of assuming the worst when
we see a homeless person downtown," I murmur, hoping he'll
continue.

"We sat and talked for over an hour, James is a veteran,
no family, a horribly sad history, including a long battle
with alcoholism. It only took me an hour to be invested
enough to help him get back on his feet. Now James is
still painting beautiful, haunting portraits, but they are on
enormous canvases." Nick glances at me reddening slightly, as
if he's said too much.

"You're like, the best fairy godmother *ever*," the words pop
out of my mouth, and I'm happy when he laughs. We keep
eating in comfortable silence. I cannot even believe this man.
Who is this perfect? He's built like a god, he's kind, he loves
art, he listens to great music, he loves good food and he helps
the homeless? *Seriously, all he needs is a kitten rescued from a
gutter and women's clothes will just start to fall off randomly when
he walks in a room.*

While I'm marvelling at how perfect he is and how much I
wish I had Veronica's trust fund so that I could charm my way

13

into his gallery, then his heart, and then his bed, he clears his throat.

"So, this morning Veronica told me she can't make the opening," he says gruffly, looking at me. I meet his eyes, not sure how to respond, because, my inner voice is screaming, *I know, and I'm glad, she's a snotty bitch and I have no idea why you waste time with her outside of selling her paintings she doesn't actually appreciate and I sincerely hope those ruby red lips of hers have never been anywhere near your skin because it doesn't matter how much money she has she is wrong for you, and I wish I was right because you are amazing and gaaaahhhh,* which doesn't seem appropriate.

Luckily he continues. "I had actually lined up Williams' daughter, Laurel, as a replacement, this is just the kind of event where people are more at ease if I'm not a single guy alone. Apparently I'm not very 'approachable'." He shrugs and continues, "So here's the thing, Laurel has a flight tomorrow very early and she'd rather not go…so I was wondering if you would like to come instead."

Hoping to hell that my face is doing a good job of hiding the fireworks that just went off in my brain and lit the butterflies in my stomach on fire, I stare at him for a moment.

"Yes, I could do that."

His face clears and he smiles, "Great. Of course I will pay for your time."

Shut up.

"If you'd like, this afternoon go ahead and use the credit card,"

Shut up.

"Get something to wear, whatever you need,"

Ohmygod shut up.

"It's kind of formal, evening wear, unless you have something...?" He trails off uncomfortably, so I keep my smile plastered on my face because, no, I don't actually have evening wear. Also his offer, while awkward as all hell and making me feel like a hooker, is generous and being made because he is kind.

"That's really nice of you Mr. Mason, I'm going to take you up on that, when would you like me ready to go?"

He gives a relieved sigh that I'm not supposed to hear.

"I'll see you at seven, and Breanna, could you please call me Nick?"

"Only if you call me Bree...all my friends do." He looks surprised for a moment and then nods.

"Fair enough, Bree."

I smile, astonished at my own boldness and this crazy turn of events, and get up from the table. As I gather lunch dishes and head to the sink, I hear his chair shift back as well, and glance over my shoulder. His eyes catch mine with a tiny flicker of guilt, as he rips them away from staring at my butt.

So glad I can turn to the dishes and the sink because, once again, stupid blushing, my smile widens and I allow myself a teeny tiny dream about how tonight might end.

Fancy...for Work

❦

Bree

T he black credit card is burning a hole in my pocket and I swear if I have one more flashback to those old 80s movies where two people from different worlds collide and magically fall in love and everything turns out perfect, I am going to spontaneously combust. As I leave the loft to get ready 'for the ball' *internal giggle, carnal reference to balls, stop it Bree,* I realize I have absolutely zero idea where to go and what to buy for a gallery opening.

Sitting on the subway heading to the heart of the shopping district, I am starting to panic. I can't just walk into some store and figure this shit out, I am a jeans and t-shirt girl. I like my jeans tight and my t-shirts to show off a little cleavage. If I'm being fair I would describe myself as pretty with a small helping of trashy. I am pretty sure I will die if I actually have to Google what to wear. It's time to call Margo.

Margo is my aunt on my mother's side who is closer to me in age, 36 to my 25. She's also my best friend. She is fearless, pulls no punches, and she will *absolutely* pretend she knows what I should buy. I sigh as I text her because the other side of this is all the questions I'm going to have to answer.

Me: 911 I need you to come help me shop

Margo: Holy crap you just played my song, what we shopping for?

Me: Gallery opening, for work, fancy

Margo: stop, did mr perfect ask you out, i swear to gawd you better spill

Me: NO it's just for work, Veronibitch is on a boat somewhere and his backup fell thru that's it now come help me

Margo: uh-huh. Fine, see you at Miros in 30

Me: Miros...omg I'm gonna barf

Margo: shut up, we'll make him forget this is work

Me: LOL still gonna barf see ya there

Smiling, I put my phone away and try to breathe myself into some semblance of calm. Margo is on the job.

It's a Date...Right?

Nick

Wʜat possessed me to ask Breanna...*Bree* to the gallery opening? Laurel was fine with going...there is no flight. I am an idiot.

I lean into the counter in my bathroom, hands on the granite, stare into the mirror, and force myself to admit that I asked her because she interests me. She was right there with me when I was telling her James' story, she got tears in her eyes when I told her what I know of his past, she was thrilled to hear that he is changing his life. I didn't even tell her that I won't gain anything from this particular show. I'm not actually going to charge him a commission on this one, Williams is going to kill me, but all James needs is a chance.

Bree has only been here a few months and it feels like I've

known her for a long time. She's quiet, but I think that's just because *I'm* quiet and she's trying to act the way she thinks I want her to act. Sometimes I wish I could just ask her what she's thinking. Sometimes I wish I could just kiss her. *Shit.*

The first day she came, she got here early. I didn't hear her, the music was loud and I was pushing through a hard workout. I headed to the kitchen for a water and when I turned she was just there, long blonde hair, kind of wavy, that she'd tamed back into a loose messy knot, little tendrils escaping to lay along her neck; her long neck that led down to a crisp white blouse with one extra button popped open, showing off just a hint of the curve of her breasts.

I forced myself to focus on her face and that didn't help either, full lips that smiled easily, lightest dusting of freckles across her pale skin, and clear green eyes with gold flecks. She had these gold hoop earrings in, and for some reason they were about the sexiest things I had ever seen, mixed in with that blonde hair curling down her neck. Wondering what the hell was wrong with me staring like a horny teenager, I talked to her for a few minutes so she wouldn't think I was an ass, and bailed.

Over the next couple of months we ate together whenever I was in town, and I learned more about Breanna. Her big family that she couldn't talk about without a smile and a funny story. How much she had loved culinary school and how someday she'd like to open her own place. The girl had goals, and she was so real, so funny, so easy to talk to, but I didn't make a move.

She was too good for me, too far away from my life, someone like Veronica would chew her up and spit her out. Bree is sunny and sassy and perfect. I have a laundry list of defects according to the very short list of women I've been with over the past few years, "closed off" and "cold" are some of the highlights. It's too hard to open up, I don't know what to share...I'm too certain I'll be disappointed.

At night, alone with my thoughts, I can admit that I'm afraid. My father loved my mother so fiercely, with incredible focus and intensity. When she died, it shattered him completely. My heart tells me it would be worth the risk, my brain tells me to get back to work, find love later. *If at all.*

Williams is always trying to get me to be 'more approachable'. I'm about 99% sure he engineered my meeting with Veronica. I tick the boxes for Veronica, I'm smart, I know women find me attractive, I'm wealthy, I dress well, I travel. What Veronica doesn't care about is me. She doesn't care about art unless she wants to hang it on her wall, and that's all based on the price tag. She doesn't care about what I like to do when I'm not working, she's never spent time at my loft, no one would *see* her there. My only worth to Veronica is my success and my looks.

I attend events with Veronica because I keep thinking maybe she's as good as it gets. She's beautiful, no doubt about that, glossy brown hair, perfect makeup always, I've never actually seen her without her makeup. Tall and toned, spoiled rotten. She's got money, and when she wants to, she oozes charm out of every pore. I wish I wanted her, but she has no problem leaving me high and dry for the gallery show, something she knows is important to me.

It was just a wild hare, a week ago she and her friends jumped on the boat 'Daddy' gave her and told the captain to take them somewhere fun. She called me two days later.

"Nick, darling, you should see the precious boat Daddy got

me, it's adorable," she gushed, as I shook off the deep sleep I was in at three am.

"I just wanted to let you know that I've been thinking about you." Veronica continued with a light slur to her words, "And when I get back I want us to talk about taking our relationship to the next level."

Really you spoiled brat? Really. Let's go to the next level when you just bailed on a yacht with your friends and I'm sure plenty of boy-toys lounging around? Who in real life even says the next level? Who calls a yacht adorable?

Saying none of that, I opened and shut my mouth twice before managing, "When will you be back? I was expecting you for the show."

Her voice lowered to a purr. "Oh let's not worry about your little gallery opening, I'll buy a few things when I get back. Let's talk about you *taking care of my opening.*"

All I felt was cold, nothing about this was sexy…apparently I was a pet and all she had to do was throw money at my gallery once in a while to shut me up. I grunted a quick, "whatever" into the phone and hung up, eager to get away from her, even if it was just her voice on the line.

She called again the next day, definitely more sober, not any more appealing.

"Nick, darling, you're being ridiculous, what do you want me to do, tell my friends we have to leave? Bunny has a private island and we're all getting so much sun and I just feel like I deserve a moment for myself. Do you have any idea how much pressure I'm under when I'm home, from you, from Daddy, from everything!! It's not fair Nick, I need this, I need to recharge, I deserve this, and you're being so selfish."

I actually held the phone away from my ear for a second in disbelief as she continued, "Get over this snit and don't worry baby, I've decided we've waited long enough. When I get home, we're going to bed until you can't even remember why you were mad." She laughed as if she were some amazing sex siren that I would be powerless to resist.

I ground my teeth together, my jaw flexing to the point of pain as I gritted out, "Don't bother sweetheart, you're not worth the trouble."

Wish Breanna hadn't been there to watch. Wonder how much she heard and what she thought about me after...

Shaking off the mood I'm sinking into, I call Laurel and cancel, not an issue, her schedule is always overloaded with hopefuls. I'm pretty sure she was squeezing my event in between a dinner for Williams and drinks at some club late tonight anyway. That handled, my thoughts turn back to tonight and how this not-a-date with Bree might unfold.

I wonder what she's going to buy, is she dressing for me? Or for the job? *...what is my problem, I all but insisted that this is not a date, told her I'd pay her, told her to use my card for clothes. So... I'm an asshole...no wonder her smile got funny, I treated her like a prostitute.*

Stalking out of the bathroom, I rip open my closet door and sigh. Row upon row of tailored clothing, mostly blacks and grays, hang neatly. I pause as my gaze falls on a polished wooden box on the shelf. I haven't opened it in a long time. Running my fingers over the shining maple, polished and inlaid with strips of mahogany, I finger the clasp and think about Breanna, *Bree*.

I hope she doesn't get nervous and wear black, there's enough black in my life. Picturing her, blonde hair shining, wearing something expensive, maybe blue or red, my mind wanders to what she might have on under the dress, lace? Satin? With a groan I adjust myself and decide compression shorts will be under my suit pants tonight, I'd like to get through the evening without embarrassing myself completely.

I dress and check my reflection, returning to the maple box. Opening it quickly and reaching for one of the velvet pouches inside, I put it in my suit pocket as my phone pings a text noise.

I glance at the screen and Bree's name appears, *damn it I knew this was too good to be true, she's cancelling,* I swipe it open,

Breanna: Would you like me to meet you at the gallery or at your place?

Momentarily relieved that she still wants to go, I read her words again and feel like I'm walking into a minefield. There's probably a right and wrong answer to her simple text. My first instinct is to meet her there, coming to the loft is out of her way, but maybe she wants me to arrive with her. Should I have offered to pick her up? If this was a date I would be picking her up. *What the hell is my problem, this is not a date, this is business, and I am a man for fuckssake, not some damn 15 year old with a crush...*

Me: I'll pick you up, send me your address.

Yeah, so I'm a man...with a crush. Whatever.

I Think This Might Be A Date

Bree

I stare at his reply for a long minute before Margo tugs at my hair impatiently to get me to turn.

"What's Mr. Perfect have to say?" She continues to curl and spray and pin, standing back and pursing her lips before carefully smoothing a couple of stray hairs. I haven't responded so she pauses, looking at me.

"He wants to pick me up, he asked for my address." Margo's hands freeze in mid-air as she glances at me and sees the panic creeping into my eyes. She quickly resumes the finishing touches on my hair, a knowing smile on her face.

"Thought you said this wasn't a date."

"IT'S NOT. Seriously can't he read? I asked if I should meet him at the gallery or his place. I DID NOT ask him to pick me up!" While this shouldn't be a big deal, for me it really is, I don't know if I can deal with him walking into my reality. As usual, Margo reads my mind.

"Are you worried about him finding out you live in the attic of a potentially haunted house? Or are you worried he's going to figure out you're from the 'burbs'?" Margo muses, putting the final spritz of something on my hair and stepping back with a nod of satisfaction.

"It's not haunted you goof," my response is automatic and we both laugh. One of Margo's favorite pastimes is knocking my attic.

I live on the third floor of an old Victorian house that has resisted being torn down while upscale apartments and condos spring up like daisies all around it. The house sits on about 50 acres of prime real estate, complete with a creek and woods surrounding it, a nice buffer from the city.

If you were being kind you would call it elegantly dilapidated. If you were being accurate you would call it a rickety old money-pit. My landlady, Mrs. Henderson, is about 400 years old. She was born in the house and she's planning to die there. She was a nanny for the current mayor's father years and years ago, and she never lets him forget it, so she doesn't get hassled much by the city about selling off the land.

She also plays cards at the senior center with my Grandma. When I graduated and started culinary school, she offered me the attic. It's a pretty sweet deal, I do the housework that's hard for her, like vacuuming and laundry, and I run her errands once a week. In return, she lets me have ridiculously cheap rent and I get to live in this beautiful old house with free run of the amazing, *best part of the house, seriously*, kitchen.

I love the attic. It's one huge open space, windows looking

out all sides, tons of light. I'm pretty sure I'm not the first tenant as the attic's been finished enough that it has a bathroom with a huge claw-foot tub, a toilet and sink. Old plaster walls with some amazingly bad floral wallpaper, some of them even sporting remnants of velvet flocking, make me wonder if this old house has a bit of a scandalous history.

* * *

My family lives in the suburbs, my mom is a music teacher, my dad is a mechanic. The house I grew up in is your standard ranch style, suburban cookie cutter place. Full of love, but with five kids, also full of people.

At 25 I'm the oldest, next are the twins Anthony and Andrew. They're 22, finished community college with automotive training and now they're busily helping my Dad expand the shop. My next brother, Nathan, is 19, he joined the military and is going to be heading to college soon, he wants to get his EMT and train for something medical.

And finally there's Clarissa. We all call her Clary. She's the darling of the family, well protected with three older brothers. She's 17, a junior in high school, a younger, sweeter version of me, wide-eyed and friendly.

I read the text from Nick again as if I will be able to squeeze new information out of those eight little words.

"I just want a chance to really get to know him. I mean, I've been working for him for almost a year, and this is the first chance I've gotten to see him outside of his apartment." I huff out a frustrated sigh. "Do you think he just wants to see where I live? Just curiosity?" I ask Margo, meeting her eyes in the big old gilt mirror I found in a corner when I moved in and propped up against the wall.

"I don't know Sugarpop, maybe he's just being a gentleman?" She smiles and turns me to face her, giving me a gentle tap on the chest. "You just need to *be you*. Stop thinking he's too good, don't worry about what he thinks of the house, if this isn't a date, what do you care anyway?" Margo stares at me as if daring me to throw all my feelings out in a pile for her to pick through.

"You're right, and I don't, this is just work." We both know I'm lying, but she nods and turns to grab my dress. I quickly text Nick my address and toss my phone on the bed. I avoid Margo's eyes as I drop my robe.

I'm not ashamed of my body, far from it, I'm 5'6" with a small waist and good curves. I bike and run and work outside when I can, helping with the property to stay in shape.

The reason I avoid Margo's eyes is the same reason she lets out a pervy whistle, causing me to laugh and blush.

"Mmm mm MMM! Look at you all matchy-matchy, not a date, my ass..." Margo trails off in a peal of giggles.

Normally if I have to wear a dress, I throw on whichever bra works best with the neckline and a thong so there's no lines. Today I made an extra stop and threw my own card down on a bra and panty set, complete with honest-to-goodness garters and silk stockings. This dress just won't work with bare legs and non-matching underwear, it's too special.

Margo unzips the garment bag and carefully takes out the dress. We both let out a little sigh.

"It's beautiful," I can't stop the smile from stretching my lips. I have never owned anything this nice in my entire life, and it is all Margo's doing.

"It's the girl that makes the dress, not the other way around Sugarpop, you're going to be the belle of the ball," Margo smiles, holding it out for me to slip into and carefully zipping the back.

I went into the store figuring I would try a couple things on, pick something classy and elegant and hopefully not too crazy expensive. Probably black, right? Don't people wear black for evenings?

Nope. Margo put the hammer down on the first black dress I pulled out.

"How washed out and sad are you hoping to look tonight?" she asked, handing the black dress off to one of the staff and shaking her head.

Glancing quickly through the rack, she pulled three dresses and sent me back to try them on while she looked to see if there was anything else she missed.

"Come out and let me see each one, you never know til the dress is off the hanger and on your body," she preached as I grumbled my way to the dressing room.

I put on the first dress, an emerald green cocktail dress that kind of gathered at the side of my waist. It was pretty but the neckline was damn near to my belly button. Not the look I was going for, so I gave her a quick peek and peeled it off. The next one was a sleeveless navy sheath, beautiful satiny fabric, square neckline and some sort of bow detailing along the hem.

"Oh hell, I didn't see the bows, no, take it off," Margo griped, I started to argue because this was *for work*, the navy was classy and safe and probably what I was supposed to be looking for right?

"Shut up. Put on the last one, I've got a good feeling," she snapped, so I gave up and slid the third dress on...and damn. She was right.

A Mansion in the Woods

Nick

*H*oping my jeep's GPS isn't completely leading me astray, I turn up a tree-lined drive, long enough that I can't even see the house. It's almost sunset, and the light through the trees is amazing. It's a beautiful spring evening, and as I round the curve of the driveway the house comes into view.

Calling it a house is misleading, it's a sprawling Victorian-era mansion that has seen better days. But under the general need for paint and repair, it has the most amazing details. I stand there for a moment, admiring some of the hand-carved workmanship around the front window and up onto the porch, when the door opens and there she stands.

Bree is perfection. Her hair is swept up into some kind

of twist that looks effortless and elegant. Flawless makeup, unnecessary, but it only accentuates her beauty. She's wearing simple diamond studs and a thin gold bracelet circles one wrist. Her slender hands give away her nerves as they tightly hold a small gold clutch. And her dress. I can't avoid smiling broadly as I take in her dress and look into those clear green eyes.

Her dress is the most beautiful scarlet I have ever seen, raw silk with rough edges, Areas at the hip, rib cage and back have been cut out and replaced with lace dyed the same color. The cut is simple, ending just a fraction above her knees and hugs her curves perfectly.

"I'm so glad you didn't pick black, I was afraid you might." I step closer and offer my elbow for the walk down the steps to my jeep. *Why did I say that, I can't just say, "nice dress", "you look amazing"? Dammit.*

"Oh, I headed for black, I'm not very brave, but you can thank my friend Margo for steering me to this." She laughs lightly and takes hold of my arm.

"I'll do that," I smile as we reach the jeep and she gracefully hops on the seat. As she swings her legs in, I get a full view of sexy legs encased in silk stockings ending in a brushed gold pump. As she turns to the side to put her wrap and clutch on the backseat, her skirt rides up a little and I glimpse the ends of her garter's white lace straps. *Shiittttt. This woman will ruin me.*

Shutting the door I compose my face and stop thinking about her legs and that lace. *That's a lie, I can't think about anything else.*

* * *

"Tell me how you came to live in such an amazing house." Bree smiles at my words, and the drive to the gallery is pleasant. She relaxes as she tells me about Mrs. Henderson and some of the history of the home.

Conversation with her is effortless, and I think of the times I've been in a car with Veronica. Of course, it wasn't my jeep, Veronica has a car and driver at her disposal, and most of our time spent travelling to and from an event or the clubs consisted of her and her idiot friends gossiping and screaming for more champagne.

On the extremely rare occasions that we were alone in the car, Veronica divided her time equally between giving me instructions concerning who to talk to and giving the driver instructions to make sure we were seen, especially by the paparazzi, at her best angle as she exited.

I sigh and Bree jumps slightly, her lovely cheeks coloring, "I'm sorry, I must be boring you to death."

"No, quite the opposite actually, I was just thinking that this was the most I have enjoyed a car ride with a woman in a very long time." I pause, wondering if she is going to take this next bit the way that I hope.

"If you don't mind, could you open the glove box? I brought you something to wear for tonight, er, if you want to of course." I trail off lamely, but she actually looks a little excited as she pops open the latch and sees the small velvet pouch. Carefully loosening the strings, she tips it up and the necklace I brought spills into her hand.

Unwinding the chain and holding it up, she gasps, "Oh um... oh my...is this real?" referring to the large diamond drop hanging off the delicate chain.

Chuckling, I enjoy her reaction, "Yes, it was my mothers, she had quite a collection."

"It's amazing," she breathes, as I pull up to the valet at the gallery. Lightly grasping her elbow to stop her from getting out of the jeep just yet, I reach for the necklace. She hands it to me and turns away, offering me the chance to stare at the curve of her neck, her delicate ears, and the beautiful line of her jaw, as I gently fasten the clasp. My fingers graze her neck, and I almost expect to see sparks from the sudden heat. I linger for just a moment, breathing in her perfume.

Bree is still and quiet, and I clear my throat the tiniest bit, "Shall we head inside?"

She glances over her shoulder, giving me a sassy grin, "We shall."

The Cream Puff Fiasco

Bree

*I*t is *so* hard not to reach up to my throat every five
seconds to check that the diamond nestled in the hollow
of my throat is still there. It feels like it's the size of a
golf ball. *This man has me well and truly scrambled.*

His reaction to the dress was perfect, *thank you Margo,* and
I find myself wondering if he got in on the 'accidental' flash
of garter as I got in the jeep. Smiling, I yank my hand away
from the necklace yet again and follow him through the front
door of the gallery. It's empty except for the wait staff who
are prepping the trays of small bites and champagne. They
efficiently and quietly move through the gallery, getting their
jobs done, and I take a minute to look around.

Nick notices and slows his pace, "The space is divided into

two sections, with the front divided again, so that if you turn to the right, I feature a small permanent collection." I take in the large white walls and carefully placed divider screens anchored by thin chains to ceiling and floor, "To the left is always an unknown local artist, someone I'm hoping to promote that probably wouldn't get the exposure otherwise." I smile and nod, silently encouraging him to continue.

"As we come to the center, I leave this entire area open for the feature collection, this changes about every six months. This is James' work." I step through a large archway and stop in my tracks. I hear Nick's pleased laugh behind me as I try to take in the canvases on the gallery walls.

"I had almost the same reaction you're having right now, and I was only seeing what James could do on pieces of cardboard with bits of charcoal he pulled from old fires. I can't imagine seeing them for the first time on canvas at this scale." Nick falls silent, giving me a moment to take it all in.

I walk slowly over to the first picture, it looks like there are about twelve canvases total. Honestly there wouldn't be room to display more and do them justice, giving them the space they deserve. The smallest canvas is probably three feet wide and five feet tall. The largest has to be at least eight feet by maybe 10 or 12 wide. All black and white, James has done portraits that are so close to the person that only their face, most of their hair, and maybe a hint of their clothing can be seen.

"The detail is amazing, I stand here feeling like I could stare all day and still find things," I whisper. I'm not sure if it's been a minute or an hour that I've been mesmerized by the soulful faces in these portraits, but I feel his heat behind me right before his hand gently touches my shoulder, strong and hot,

"Tell me what you see," he says quietly, close enough that I feel the flutter of his breath on my ear.

"He's captured the very essence of them hasn't he," I begin quietly, "The sadness, the madness, the burden that life has thrown at them." I pause and he waits, so I continue.

"I think through all that, what strikes me the most is their eyes. Not a single one of these people has lost hope. There is still joy in being alive, through the sadness shines determination, through the pain you see the will to survive. These are really powerful." I take a tiny step away so I can turn to face Nick without bumping into him.

He lets his hand fall back to his side lightly and looks at me for a long second before dropping his head, scruffing his hand through his beard.

"Five minutes and you see all that too. I'm glad you're here Bree, I'm glad you got to see this. He's really something huh?"

"He's more than something, it's like he picks you up and drops you right into the middle of their soul and all you can do is fall because it's not about feeling sorry for them, it's about seeing them as humans, not homeless problems..." I taper off, embarrassed. *He is staring at me. I think he's closer to me. He's looking at my lips. His eyes are so dark. Please kiss me.*

He leans a tiny bit closer and I feel his breath mingle with mine, I let my lips part just slightly and my eyes start to slide closed,

"Nick, darling!"

No, no-no-no-NO, my eyes snap open, I take a quick step back and turn and there she is, Veroni*bitch* striding through the archway, tossing her coat at one of the staff as if he isn't trying to carry a tray full of glasses to the bar. She's in black *ha!* silk, dripping with opals, her brown hair shining in loose waves past her shoulders.

Nick turns, and I see disappointment mingling with the surprise on his face before he smooths it into bland indifference.

"Hello V, I didn't think you were going to grace us with your presence this evening," disdain is heavy in every word, his eyes are hooded. *He's not happy to see her! I want to dance! I want to sing! I will do neither, I will be cool!*

"Oh don't be silly, of course I was coming, don't you and I enjoy these little jokes?" appearing to notice me for the first time, Veroni*bitch* leans towards me and gives me a conspiratorial elbow and a wink, "Adds to the chase, and just look at the prize." *When she smiles she looks like a viper, does she think he can't hear her, what do I say? PRIZE? Can I slap her? I really kind of think a good slap would do her some good. Better not.*

Smiling my best *fall off a cliff* smile, I turn to Nick.

"I just have to make a quick phone call, will you excuse me for a minute?" I pretend not to notice as Veroni*bitch's* eyes widen and then narrow speculatively as her gaze lingers on the diamond nestled to my throat.

"Sure, I need to have a few words with Veronica anyway," he turns completely away from her, ignoring her little sniff of annoyance, and his gaze softens. "You can use my office just down the back hall, first door on the right, there's more to see when you get back," leaning close to my ear, his lips brush my cheek and he whispers, "thanks again for not choosing black."

Inclining my head at both of them in what I hope is a graceful nod, I ignore the lightning bolt that just started at my heart and rocketed straight to my nether regions as I turn and walk down the hall.

I can feel two pairs of eyes boring into me, hopefully he is watching the sway of my hips *that'd piss her right off.* I find the door and step into his office, shutting it carefully behind me before leaning against it, trying to get a handle on the moment.

Taking a deep breath and blowing it out slowly, I pull my phone out of the ridiculous tiny purse, also courtesy of Margo.

Me: this night just took a weird turn

Me: let's start with the art is freaking amazing

Me: but here's the thing, Veroni*bitch* just showed up

Me: and right before she did I am pretty sure he was going to kiss me

Me:...

I huff out a sigh and look around the room. I can tell it's his, he didn't have someone just decorate for him, he's made the space his own. A large desk dominates one side of the room, gleaming wood, black leather executive chair. The other side has a large Persian rug that's probably worth my rent for five years. A few nice pieces of furniture in tweed and leather and lamps placed so that he doesn't have to rely on harsh overhead light to complete the space. I can imagine him discussing gallery events with clients or business with Williams, *I don't have to call him Mr in my head,* here.

I glance at the clock, wondering if I've given Nick enough time to talk to Veronica, and my phone pings.

Margo: okay this is too much for me to process, what's she doing now?

Me: don't know i told him i needed to make a call

Margo: WHAT

Me: what?

Margo: can you see them at least? details

Me: no, I'm in his office
Margo: idiot. GO LOOK
Me: cripes fine

I open the door casually and lean against the wall beside it, holding my phone up to my ear so I can pretend I'm talking as I carefully glance down the hall. Nick is mostly turned away, but the set of his back does not say happy. Veronica is right in his face, volume rising, her red lips twisted and ugly.

"...how long do you expect me to stand here, the media hasn't even arrived..." Nick growls something I can't hear and her eyebrows climb up to her hairline.

"Leave? I assume you mean have the car do a few laps so that we can down a bottle of champagne and come back later? ... What?...Who's Bree?" Her head swivels around looking down the hall at the office and I jerk my gaze away and focus on my fake phone call.

"Is that the little *mouse* I saw in your kitchen when I stopped by last week before drinks? Oh my *god* Nick, I thought she was here to...I don't know...take coats? Help people find the toilets?" Veronica pauses for effect. "Is. *She.* Your. Date?"

Complete disbelief? Check. Outraged affronted expression? Check. *I hate her so much right now.* She is staring at Nick like he has sprouted tentacles from his face. I'm squeezing my phone so hard it actually creaks alarmingly. *Is he going to stand up for me? Do I want him to? Yes, duh. I completely regret missing the opportunity to slap her earlier. Please Nick say something.*

After an overly long pause, she dissolves into laughter. Cruel, cold, haughty laughter, and I am about to take off my heels and throw down out there, *that's a lie, I would have no idea what to do besides slap her, I just watch too much reality TV,* when Nick leans forward, right in her face, and growls something.

I would give up a lesser used body part to hear what he said to her, because her laughter cuts off like he hit the mute button and she takes two steps back, her hands flying up to her mouth in shock. They stand that way for another long second and I watch the color flood her face as her expression morphs from shock to rage.

Crack! The sound of her hand connecting with his cheek is sharp and sudden, rocking his head back ever so slightly, she raises her hand as if she's going to hit him *again*, but I've had enough. This spoiled little brat is *not* going to ruin his night.

"Well look at that, one little phone call and I miss all the fun," I drawl lazily as I stroll down the hall, heavy sway in my step, not a care in the world, *holy crap, mad Me is a sultry minx...I like her.*

Veroni*bitch* swings around, staring at me for several full seconds before composing her face, total ice princess. She looks me over, and it's a full-on appraisal that I obviously fail. I can tell she'd like to grab my jaw and look at my teeth like a damn race horse, so I bare them at her and pretend it's a gracious smile as Nick puts a hand on my waist to steer me away.

"Enough, Veronica," he growls and she once again morphs her face. Like magic she has a tiny chin quiver, big luminous eyes, and she's staring right at him, shyly reaching out one hand.

"You didn't mean that did you Nick? After *all* we've been through? Let's go out to the car and talk, take a minute to reset, I've missed us." She carefully sucks her lower lip between her teeth, *damn she's good,* and looks at him expectantly.

It's not working. Nick has a look on his face like thunder,

and her reaching hand falters.

"There is no us. There never really was. See yourself out Veronica."

His hand doesn't leave my waist, and he tightens his grip slightly to lead me back to the center of the gallery. An attendant has magically appeared with Veronica's coat and she tears it out of his hands and steps closer to me.

"Smile all you want you silly bitch, you're obviously too stupid to see he's tarted you up just to play games with me," she hisses in my ear. "What could *you* possibly have to offer him when he could have had *me*?" Turning, she stalks toward the door, her heels a loud staccato on the smooth floors.

With herculean effort I maintain my best smile, turn away from her and allow Nick to steer me away for just a second, before my brain short circuits and...*nope, can't just let that go, be right back, please don't fire me.*

I take three quick steps to the bar and with a quick look, grab one of the trays.

"Oh Veronica," I coo loudly to get her attention. "You're leaving so soon you didn't have a chance to taste any of the delicious snacks!" I would love to frisbie the tray at her, but I don't actually want to hurt her, so I give the tray a hard flick keeping tight hold of the edge. Every one of the 35 or so adorable little cream puffs on tiny papers fly off the tray. At least 15 of them hit the mark, stuck to her back and ass like little barnacles.

I ignore her affronted screech, turn on my heel, deposit the tray on the bar with an apologetic glance at the startled attendant, and turn back to look at her with crossed arms, waiting for the fall out. *Bitch called me a tart.*

Yanking her phone from her clutch, Veronica changes

direction, storming towards the back of the gallery.

"Daniel!" She screeches into the phone, "pick me up at the back entrance immediately!" Without another look at either of us, she rips her coat out of the hovering attendant's hands and storms down the hall. In the quiet that follows, the magical wait staff appear and quietly clean up sad little left behind cream puffs, poorly hidden smiles on their faces. I bask in the glory of my bad-assedness for another second, then I look at Nick.

His face grim, he walks over to me and once again puts his hand, hot and strong on my waist, firmly guiding me down the hall to his office. *Crap.*

Time To Take a Chance

Nick

Bree walks with me quietly, and she appears to be thinking hard, those beautiful green eyes have deepened to emerald with the weight of her anger. As we enter the office, she stops and shuts the door by leaning her back against it and holds up one finger.

"I'm not sorry, so I won't pretend, and if you're mad I can just call a cab." She announces defiantly.

This woman. How could Veronica have called her a mouse? She is a lioness, she is golden. She is amazing. *And let's not forget the cream puffs.* As I shake off the abstraction that her very presence puts me under, I relive the last few minutes.

Laughter bursts out of my chest, full and loud. The look on

Veronica's face as someone not only dared to put her in her place, but did so with such flair is my undoing. Bree stares at me for a split second and then she is laughing too, the kind of laughter that is so infectious, just looking at each other sends us off again. I walk over to the desk and sit on the edge, still laughing, but softer now, as my scattered thoughts catch up to me and I realize that this is my chance.

Since I hired her, I've avoided being anything other than Bree's boss. I pay her well, I stay out of her way, I'm distant and quiet during our meals together, often cursing the moment of weakness that prompted me to ask her to dine with me in the first place. It would be easy to disregard my attraction for her with a trite, 'we don't have much in common', but the conversations with her just come too easy for that to be true.

My head tells me that she's wrong for me. I work too much, I like my privacy, I'm used to being alone. Bree would be a square peg in the round hole that is my life. Over the past few months, when the temptation to just ask her out and see what happens was almost too much, my brain mercilessly decided she's too young. Not just in years, I think she's in her mid twenties, *so there's a gap but not a canyon.* Bree just exudes this quality of innocence. Youthful, exuberant, *sassy,* happiness that makes me feel serious and jaded.

Other times, though, when we talk, it feels so fucking right I just want to tangle my fingers in her hair and see if her lips are as soft as they look against my own. A small voice in my heart starts whispering then, telling me that maybe she's exactly what I need.

I realize that Bree has stopped laughing and is watching me. Looking up into her clear green eyes, I blow out a sigh that holds all my fears and listen to that little voice, this one time.

Here goes nothing.

"I wish I knew how to keep you out of my head," my voice has gone deep with nerves, her eyes widen and I look down at my hands. I want her to know, once, how I feel.

"I tried to keep this professional, ignore how I'm feeling, but I'm tired, Bree," pausing, I glance at her face. Bree's got one lip trapped between her teeth, staring at me, and I can't tell what she's thinking. *I need to get to the fucking point.*

"I'm asking if you want to try…being more?" *Well I'm clearly not a fucking poet.* Spreading my hands in front of me, I shrug, hoping she'll say something.

Knock, knock, knock. A diffident tapping on the door breaks the brief silence. I stand up from the desk edge, expressionless as Bree gives a startled little gasp and then visibly settles herself, turns and opens the door.

"Sir? James has arrived as well as several members of the media who would like a few words with you both before the gallery opens." The head waiter glances between us, unsure if he is interrupting something before I nod and he quickly walks back down the hall.

Bree hasn't moved, and she isn't looking at me. *I should have said nothing. I am a fool.* I clear my throat and head for the door.

"It's time to start the show," I pause just past her, "I'm sorry I said anything, I should have let things be," I whisper.

I freeze as her hand closes over my wrist, butterfly wings with a core of steel.

"Nick, wait."

My eyes close, I don't want to dare to hope.

Her hand gives an insistent shake on my wrist, and I open my eyes, focusing on her lips as her next words spill out in a jumble, breathy and low.

"This is a lot, and I...*wow*...I want to just talk to you so much right now, but you've got to get out there, and talking would be a waste because *here's* what I really want to do. It's a promise for later. I'm sorry I sound like a moron." Bree huffs at herself impatiently and raises up on her tiptoes, her hands slip behind my neck and she's kissing me.

Her lips are full and soft, pressing hard against my own and when I feel the flick of her tongue, I deepen the kiss. My hands slide around her waist, registering the heat of her skin, the thin layer of silk, the way she fits against my body. *This is Bree, kissing my lips, filling my nose with her jasmine perfume. Mine.*

Bree pulls back with a little sigh, her eyes searching mine. I lean down, kissing her once more, then hold her close as I feel her breath on my neck.

"You probably better not let them wait too long out there, Nick," her voice is muffled and I feel her lips brush across my skin.

"They'll be fine," I grumble, tightening my arms for a moment. Bree gives a sexy little laugh and puts her hands on my chest, pushing lightly.

"Either that waiter or I will die of embarrassment if he has to knock on that door again...so in the interest of me or the waiter not dying, go do the show." She smiles archly, "Don't worry, I take promises seriously."

"Woman...," I exhale, kissing those full lips once more, softly. Then, taking her hand, we walk out to the gallery together.

Better Than a Daydream

Bree

The night is a blur of utter perfection, Nick is at my side, hand on my waist, smoothly introducing me as Bree, no other title needed, and it feels wonderful. The fact that he isn't saying, "my friend Bree" makes me something more. I'm so overwhelmed that more than anything I wish I could take five minutes, go somewhere quiet and just dump all my feelings out and look them over.

I kissed Nick Mason.

All of my daydreams came true in that one kiss, and *mmmmm*, did that man kiss me back. My heart starts fluttering and my cheeks pink up slightly just thinking about it. I glance at Nick to find him watching me, he smiles a secret smile just for me as if he can tell exactly what I'm thinking. I smile back shyly and he holds out a hand, leading me over to the bar.

"Penny for your thoughts," he whispers, motioning to the bartender for two glasses of champagne. I smile and then look at him seriously.

"How long have I been in your head, Nick?"

"Since the first time I laid eyes on you, all that blonde hair knotted up in a ball on your neck, green eyes staring straight into my soul. I was done at that moment," he smiles glancing at me. *He has no idea what he does to me, every nerve in my body just did a cartwheel.*

Drinks in hand we continue to circulate, everyone wants a minute of his time. I get to spend several minutes talking to James, congratulating him on his immense talent. He is so humble and grateful to Nick for the opportunity.

"Just think Bree, no other gallery in the city would take the time to look at me or my work, much less offer me a show for no gain," James says quietly.

"No gain?" I question. "Well surely with the exposure for the gallery and commissions on sales, you both stand to gain from tonight, James."

"No, that's the thing, he won't take commission, says I can use this first show to get on my feet, make my mark on the art community…I don't know why this luck fell in my lap, Bree," James whispers, smiling. He glances over my shoulder and his smile widens just as I feel heat at my back and know Nick is there.

Turning my head up to look in his eyes, I don't know how to say what I'm feeling, so I settle for, "You sir, are amazing."

The Night is Still Young

Nick

The night finally winds down, the show was a wild success, discreet reserved markers already claim four of James' works. The catering staff are finishing loading their equipment into two vans outside the back entrance.

Bree has pulled a chair from the front reception area and I find her sitting in the center of the main gallery, eyes on the portraits. Her shoes are on the floor beside the chair and I'm sure she's tired. It's late and I'm ready to take her home. Walking up behind her, I touch her shoulder lightly. She smiles and puts her hand over mine.

"I just wanted to see them all again before they head to their new homes, his talent is amazing." She stretches gracefully and stands, stepping into her shoes. The simple movement is like ballet, the line of her leg as she points her toes to step into the heels, the arch of her back as she stands. Suddenly I can't get her in the jeep soon enough, I want her somewhere private, I want my hands on her body, I want to make her sigh and moan. Our eyes meet and I don't know what she sees in mine, but her eyes darken with desire and she slides an arm around my waist as we walk outside.

As I open the car door for her, she turns to face me and shimmies her butt up on the seat but doesn't turn and bring her legs in right away. I step in closer, my hips between her thighs and lean in to kiss her hungrily. She plants her hands on the seat behind her and arches to meet me. Her heat is burning into me everywhere we touch. *This woman has me undone.*

Breaking the kiss with a gasp, she laughs shakily. "Take me home Nick, we're wearing entirely too many clothes for what I want you to do to me." I groan into her hair, still pressed against her and nod. Walking around to my side of the jeep and getting in, I rest a hand on her knee, lightly stroking the silk stockings.

"These you're going to need to leave on for a while though, Love," I growl, "these are special."

"Mmmmm," she sighs, "If someone would have told me what strong hands on silk feel like, I wouldn't have believed it was this good." Her eyes are closed and she's smiling. I continue slow lazy strokes from her knee to the hem of her dress, simmering with anticipation as I drive us back to the loft.

We don't speak as we walk in, without saying a word, we slow down and begin to savor this moment. She steps out of her heels at the door, dropping her clutch and wrap on a nearby chair and then she just stands and looks at me. I walk across the room and push a button on the stereo, and as the bass pulses, she laughs to hear the song that was playing the day we met in my kitchen.

Walking across the room, I reach for her waist and she leans into me, sliding her hands up my shoulders looking up at me through her lashes, lips parted. I slide my hands down to her ass as hers move to my collar, slowly working the buttons as we sway to the music.

My heart stutters as she leans closer and I feel the first feather light kiss on my chest, she continues to open my shirt, kissing and nipping at my skin as I close my eyes and let her explore. She pushes the shirt off my shoulders and it drops to the floor. She stops kissing me for a moment and I feel her finger tracing the largest of my tattoos.

Bree leans forward again, I feel her tongue flick out and lick my chest before her lips press to my skin and she sucks in, lightly using her teeth to mark me. My body responds wildly, one of my hands knots in her hair, the fancy twist unravelling, the other on her back, stroking, bringing her in closer and her face back up to mine, claiming her mouth, kissing her deep and long.

Our bodies mesh and all I can feel is the heat wherever we touch. I bring my knee between her thighs and with a tiny gasp she steps her feet apart to accommodate me, her small hands sliding up my chest to my shoulders and around my neck.

We break apart just enough to breathe, foreheads touching, her eyes are closed, lips parting in a tiny smile.

That tiny smile is all the warning I get as her hands smoothly pull the band from my hair and it falls forward onto my shoulders, brushing both of our cheeks. Feeling her fingers weave through the heavy waves at the back of my neck, I lose all control and I'm kissing her again. Her lips, her jaw, the curve of her neck as she tilts her head and her breath comes faster. My hands glide over her rib cage and I run my thumb over the hard bead of her nipple, straining against the silk dress. She gasps and one of her hands slides down my chest, hovering at my belt before sliding lower over the raging hard-on that's pressed against her belly. She squeezes gently, and I groan in the hollow of her neck.

Sliding my hands around to her back, I find the zipper of her dress and pull it down gently. She lifts her shoulders lightly and the dress falls off her shoulders, I feel one hand and then the other unwind from my hair as she takes them out of the dress and it falls to her waist. I push the dress to her hips and let it fall to the floor. Her skin is golden in the dim light and the white lace that she is wearing glows. She looks like an angel.

Claiming her lips again, I feel her hands smoothly unbuckle my belt and my pants slide to the floor. Breaking the kiss, she glances down and cocks an eyebrow at the compression shorts, I laugh.

"See what you do to me? I can't think straight, much less stay in control when I'm near you," I growl. Kicking off shoes and socks, stepping out of the pants, I lower the damn shorts and let her look at me.

"Wow," she whispers on a breath with a smile. I do not deserve this woman but I will do anything to be her man. I take her hand and lead her into the bedroom.

51

Oh, My, Yes...

Bree

The day I saw Nick after his workout did not prepare me for exactly how delicious he is naked. *Or exactly how big...yay!* He's strong and in control, he knows what he wants and I know how bad I want to give it to him.

Nick walks into the bedroom, not giving up my hand until we reach the bed. He turns and sits on the edge, reaching for me. I step up to him and his hands circle my waist, pulling me close as he buries his face in my neck and kisses his way between my breasts. His hands slide up my rib cage and I feel his thumbs graze each of my nipples as I let my head fall back and give myself up to the sensation. His hands follow the line of my bra around my back and he unhooks it carefully, sliding it off my shoulders and tossing it to the side.

"I want to see you," he rumbles, hooking his thumbs in the sides of my panties, he slides them off my hips, *thank the stars I was an optimist and put them over the garters, I am a genius,* to my ankles as I step out of them and he tosses them to the side with the bra.

Laying gentle kisses across my belly he works his way up. I feel his tongue flick over my skin, sending an overload of stimulation straight to my brain as one of my hands grasps his shoulder and the other winds into his hair.

I cover his mouth with my own as I bring my knees up on the bed to either side of him, straddling him. He groans into my mouth, kissing his way down my neck again, his arms tighten around my waist, and he stands up, keeping me tight against him.

Laying me down on the bed, his lips continue in a hot trail down my stomach, he lightly snaps the belt of the garter with his teeth, his eyes full of heat as he looks up the line of my body at me.

Every nerve in my body bursts into flames as I feel his breath. He takes his time as I writhe and my nails mark his shoulders. I gasp and my thighs squeeze his head as I feel the wave rising and I shatter, my back arching, head back, he keeps his lips locked to my center, teasing and licking until I suck in a breath, collapsing back onto the bed, riding that delicious high with my eyes closed tight. He kisses his way up my body, climbing on the bed beside me.

Yes. Mine.

⤜❦⤛

Nick

*L*aying behind her, my dick pillowed against her perfect ass, I reach around and run my hand down her body. Teasing her skin as I kiss her neck, I listen to her sighs of pleasure.

I kiss her shoulder again, pushing up from the bed, smiling at her tiny whimper of protest as my fingers leave. Walking around to the nightstand, I get a condom out of the drawer and tear it open. As I turn back to the bed, Bree is sitting up and has shifted closer, crawling on hands and knees over to me, she holds out her hand. *Anything she wants.*

I hand her the condom, but she just holds it as she crawls right to the edge of the bed. Reaching out one hand, she grabs my thigh and then slides her hand around to grab the meat of my ass, pulling me towards her. Her lips part and I squeeze my eyes shut. *I'm not going to last long if she keeps doing that, god damn, I want this to last forever.*

Lost is the feel of her, suddenly I'm on the verge, *no, too soon, not yet,* and I knot my hand in her hair to hold her still, fighting my body. I open my eyes, breathing hard and look down at her. She licks her lips and her smile is full of sex, her eyes dark with lust.

"On your back," her voice is low and commanding. My body jerks with desire and I climb up on the bed, kissing her deeply as her hands push me onto my back. Her hands grip my length, and she straddles my thighs as she rolls the condom on. Bree rears up and positions over me, and my eyes want to roll straight back in my head. *Mine.*

My eyes roam her hips, the curve of her waist, her breasts swaying, her beautiful face. I meet her eyes and she stares down at me, my hands are on her hips, she's moving slow, giving her body time to stretch. She pumps up and down, pushing a little farther each time until I feel her body meet mine. Bree moans in pleasure and her hips begin to rock, forward and back, grinding our bodies together.

My hands grip her hips tightly, keeping rhythm, I lean up and claim a nipple with my lips, worrying it carefully with my teeth and she's over the edge, she loses her rhythm and begins to spasm hard and fast, moaning as she fights to keep pumping her hips.

I pull her down to my chest and roll us over, lifting my weight up off her. I push into her hard and deep as she arches, head thrown back.

"God, yes, Nick!"

I find the right angle and Bree screams her pleasure, her hips rocking with me, her nails finding my shoulders. With a final thrust I come with a groan, our bodies locked together.

As we ride the aftershocks, I lean down, kiss the swell of her breast and bury my face in the curve of her neck. She sighs, and it's a beautiful sound. I roll my weight to lay beside her and she follows, curling into my chest, our legs tangled together. She tilts her face up and I kiss her slowly, she smiles, snuggles into my side, and we sleep.

Can't Stand the Heat?

Bree

I wake up alone, the blankets tucked around me, and everything smells like Nick. I bury my face in the linens and breathe in deep, I don't even know how to describe it, but if *dark* and *serious* were translated into scents, that's Nick.

A glance at the clock tells me it's the middle of the night, so I stretch and slip off the garter and stockings with a smile. I find a robe on a hook in the bathroom and I put it on and wander down the hall to find Nick. A sensual ache between my legs makes me smile, *add sex to the list of things Nick Mason is perfect at, my bones feel like jelly, I haven't gotten off that hard in...well...ever, I thought I actually died for a second.*

Nick is in the kitchen. He's standing at the counter, his

hands gripping the edge, with his back to me. A glass of water stands untouched and his shoulders are bunched up, head down. *Shit...is he sorry he slept with me? Does he want me to leave?*

Walking up behind him, I tentatively brush a hand down his shoulder to his back, and he straightens, turns and brings his arm over my head and around my waist, tucking me into his side. I feel his lips in my hair and my worry eases up a little.

"Sorry, I didn't mean to wake you," his voice rumbles in my ear through his chest.

"No, it's fine," His skin feels like warm marble, my fingers trace the planes of his stomach, I could touch him forever.

"Do you..." he clears his throat uncomfortably, "do you want me to take you home?" I pull away as if I've been scalded, his hands drop to his sides as I look up at his face, hurt. *Hello other shoe, guess you just dropped...I am an idiot, just a one night stand... and he's trying to avoid the awkward breakfast.* I can't believe I read him so wrong, I feel angry tears welling up and turn away.

"That's okay *Mr. Mason* I'm a big girl, I can call a cab," holding the shreds of my dignity together I yank the ends of the robe belt to tighten it and storm out of the kitchen. Crossing the living room I yank open the front door and walk out to the hall, pulling it closed behind me with a thud. *And I'm barefoot... without my phone...hooray for shit planning.* I let my back thump against the wall as I hunch into the robe.

Just seconds behind me, the door is ripped open and Nick shoulders through, in his underwear, glancing between the elevator and the stairs before his eyes land on me with relief.

"You're not dressed to be out here either," I sigh, feeling a sad smile twitch the corner of my mouth.

"Don't leave," Nick blurts, moving to me quickly, his hands brushing my hair back and then hovering in the air by my arms as if he's not sure I'll let him touch me. "Please, don't leave." He repeats softly, his dark eyes searching mine.

"You basically asked me to," I whisper, feeling embarrassed and hurt.

"I…wanted to take only what you wanted to give," Nick's eyes tighten and his hands fall softly on my shoulders, gently rubbing up and down my arms. I tilt my head and give him a hard look as I mull that over. *So if I was in it for funsies he was letting me off the hook? He was hoping this was no strings attached sex?*

"I guess I'm old-fashioned," I shrug, *hoping I look cool*, "one night stands were never my thing. If that's what you thought of me…well I guess I'm bummed that I have been hardcore crushing on you for *months.*"

"You stand there, green eyes blazing at me and I want to fall in and drown, Bree." *SWOON SWOON SWOON.* "The day I met you, standing in the kitchen," Nick waves a hand back at the loft, "that was it for me. You just shine so bright I couldn't believe I might get to have you in my life. If I only got one night with you, I just…" Nick sighs, dragging his fingers through his tangled hair, "I can't do this halfway…so it seemed like maybe we should just not…" his eyes search my face and he pauses, jaw flexing.

"So you weren't even going to take a chance on me? On us?" I shake my head, feeling tears threaten again.

"God I want to," he rumbles, "you're different than anyone I've ever known. You make me feel, fuck, I don't know, you make me feel *right* Bree."

"Then reach out with both hands and grab what's right," I

challenge, shocked at my own boldness as I walk over to him, put my hands on his chest and wait until he meets my eyes, "I'm right here." I finish in a whisper.

His lips crash into mine, his hands are on my face and in my hair. Pulling me closer he unties the belt holding the robe closed and goose bumps erupt on my thighs as it falls open and his hands reach in, roaming my skin. His lips work from my mouth to my jaw to that soft spot below my ear. He nips my earlobe and I jerk, arching into him. We're moving together, my back finds the wall and I wrap my legs around his waist. He's hard and ready, pinned between us as I shift my hips, grinding against him. He pulls back for just a second, enough to shove his shorts off his hips.

"Condom," he gasps, and I can barely think straight but I shake my head.

"I'm on birth control. I want this, I want to feel you." With a low groan, he drives deep with one thrust. We both moan, my head falls back and there's nothing slow this time, nothing but need, his rhythm fast as he finds the angle and starts pounding that spot deep inside me. My vision blurs to sparkles.

"Look at me Nick, look at me, look at me, oh, oh..." His eyes meet mine, black pools of desire and I don't look away, I have just enough time.

"This, Nick, this is us," I hold his gaze as I feel the spiral take me, and staring into his eyes, I come harder than I knew was possible. The world is gone, all that remains is his eyes locked with mine as he struggles to hold on, his strokes shortening until he buries himself with a deep cry and shudders through his own release. I feel his lips moving softly on my neck as his breathing slows. Our bodies still joined, Nick reaches up and takes one of my hands, slowly moving it to rest over his pounding heart.

"Yours now," he murmurs, reaching over and opening the door, he carries me back into the loft.

She Was Here

Nick

I wake up and she's gone. I lay still for a moment replaying the night in my head. It feels like my first eight months with Bree were in slow motion and then everything went real time last night. It's hard to reconcile someone like her with my life. I feel like I've known her forever, every meal we've shared, every glance, every conversation.

I was a quiet rich kid, kept to myself, not a lot of friends. As an only child I spent more time with adults than other children, and I was much more likely to be taken to a museum or a gala than a park or camping. I don't have any complaints, I learned to appreciate art and culture, I learned to find peace in silence.

My parents were loving but distant, they traveled together for my father's business while I was raised by a fleet of nannies until I could attend the best schools. When my mother got sick, the travel stopped. She had cancer and it took her quickly, they brought me home when they knew her end was near. I was at a university at that point, ready to complete my final year. My father and I held her hands.

While there was sadness in that week, I remember it for what I learned about my parents. They were in love. My mother was everything and more to my father. He sat at her bedside, whispering an endless stream of endearments as he held her hands and kissed her fingertips. She smiled and murmured words of comfort to us both.

When my mother was gone, my father was broken. He continued his life but his spirit was gone. He called me often while I finished my final term, a welcome change, and I believe that was the one thing that brought him joy. We talked and talked about life, love, my mother, his hopes for me. I filled the void for him as much as I could, and when I graduated, I moved home to join his business.

Sanford Williams had already been my father's business partner for a number of years, and the two of them taught me how to be the best in the art world, dealing with private collectors, corporations, museums. The three of us spent many evenings of cognac and cigars in the luxurious suite my father moved into after my mother died. He couldn't bear to knock around in an empty manor, and I encouraged him to sell.

Seeing how badly the death of my mother had taken a toll on him, marriage held no appeal, and children were completely off my radar. There was no reason to save the house for me, it had never really felt like home. I found a loft downtown that suited my needs and gave me space.

For almost five years that was my life. Work, learn, sleep,

repeat. The night that I walked into my father's suite and he wasn't waiting for me in his favorite chair with a lit cigar was the worst of my life. Walking quietly through the rooms, I instinctively knew where I would find him. I called his private physician, we removed the empty bottle of whiskey, the empty bottle of pills, and the note that he left.

Find your night. It is worth it, I promise. I'm sorry. I love you.

He officially died of respiratory failure, not *a lie, he took so many pills his body forgot to breathe,* leaving me alone in the world at 29. I threw myself into my work, I traveled almost constantly, Sanford was invaluable as a partner. He held the business together, continued to build, I spent holidays with his family if I was in the city.

I dated, never serious, rarely let anyone come to the loft, refused to allow commitment in my life, never had the desire to open myself up to the pain that brought my father to his end. Love was unnecessary, connection with a woman unimportant.

Until Bree walked into my life.

My body responded to Bree the moment I saw her, my brain was slower to catch up. For weeks she was a curiosity, this bubbling, funny, beautiful woman who whirled around my loft trying very hard to fit some kind of "domestic help mode" she had concocted in her head. I spent our rare moments together observing her, listening to her stories of family and friends, enjoying her wry sense of humor, falling in love with the blush that would creep up her neck to stain her cheeks.

I sit up on the edge of the bed, and I'm almost afraid it was all a dream, I'm afraid I'll walk out there and she'll be wearing her crisp white apron, smiling her professional smile.

It was real. Bree has never been here to make me breakfast, but I smell coffee and bacon right now. I spot a small pile of lace and silk rumpled by the bed and smile as I feel a rush of heat in my chest. It was real. I pull on some clothes and head for the kitchen.

She's there, that golden hair piled up on her head, wearing my robe with the sleeves rolled up. As I watch her move, I inwardly curse myself for not watching her cook more often. She's been making exceptional food for me for almost a year now, but I've rarely been in the kitchen until it was time to eat.

My robe is so long I only get a glimpse of two cute little feet with polished red toenails as she moves through the kitchen, sure of herself. She catches sight of me and points, not to the table across the room by the windows, but at the bar stool on the opposite side of the island from where she's working. I smile as I realize sitting at the island we will be side by side. Crossing to the french press she pours a mug of coffee and brings it to me, brushing a kiss on my cheek.

"Morning," she grins, "I have to say, it was fun to already be here this morning…I've never gotten to cook you breakfast." Suddenly shy, she grabs plates from the cupboard and starts dividing up perfectly fried eggs, bacon and pan fried potatoes. *I don't want her to be shy. I don't want her to doubt last night or me.*

"I'm hoping you'll do this more often. It seems I've been missing out on more than I realized," I want to say more, but I think she hears what I mean because she smiles, pleased. Walking around the island to my side, two plates in hand, she sets one in front of me and the other at the spot beside me. Going back for silverware and her mug of coffee, she sits on the stool next to me.

We eat in companionable silence for a few minutes, then she sets down her fork and leans into my shoulder with her own.

"So I was thinking that maybe you'd like to see more of the house and the grounds where I live. Um, if you're not busy today anyway...if you are that's okay of course, I just thought... " she trails off uncertain.

"I had no plans other than hoping you wanted to spend more time together." I glance at her just in time to see relief on her face, quickly replaced by that saucy grin that is quickly becoming my favorite as her eyes meet mine.

"Fair warning, Mrs. Henderson may try to steal you away," she taps her lips thoughtfully with one finger, "I'd hate to have to throw down with my ancient landlady," she muses.

"I'll avoid her attention like a true gentleman," I give her serious face for a moment, then we share a smile and continue our breakfast. Finishing, I get up and take our plates and silverware to the dishwasher. Turning back, I watch Bree pick up both our coffee mugs. She walks over to the sink, rinses them and sets them both carefully on the counter.

"I was here," she says simply, smiling and walking down the hall.

The Beginning of 'Us'

Bree

*H*is hair is pulled back, but for the first time since I met Nick, it's not perfect which, somehow, makes him even *more* perfect. A few strands at the front are escaping and it's loose enough in the band to see some of the wave. He's wearing jeans and a dark grey t-shirt and his hand is relaxed as it holds mine during the drive, his thumb lightly stroking my wrist.

I am back in my slightly wrinkled dress, minus the stockings and garters, *although based on his reaction I will be revisiting them again, mmhmmmm.* I'm a tiny bit nervous as we turn up the long drive, I love this old house and my life here and my crotchety old landlady, but I've never shared it with anyone. I've brought my siblings and my parents here occasionally for dinner or to help Mrs. Henderson with a project I couldn't handle alone, but never a man. *My man, ohmygod.*

My mind is still whirling through last night. Having been a small part of his life for most of a year now, what started as a lusty crush had been steadily developing into feelings for him. I've wanted to know him, in every way possible, for months. To find out that he feels the same way, it's amazing.

"You've been quiet, everything okay?" His voice hums through my musings as he parks the car and turns to look at me.

"More than okay," I murmur, trying to find the words, "I was just thinking that it feels like I've known you for a long time and yet the entire beginning of "us" was last night."

"Us. I like the sound of that more every time I hear it from your lips, Bree." He turns and gets out of the jeep, rounding to my side as I open my door, meeting me before I hop off of the high seat. Stepping in close, his hips pin me in place, his hands up on the door frame he leans in, face close to mine, breath tickling my neck.

"I've never been part of a real "us" before. I never wanted to be, until I met you." His voice is low and serious and his lips meet mine gently. I slide my arms around his neck, deepening the kiss as one of his hands slides around my waist and pulls me in tight. I wrap my legs around his hips and he's lifting me, both arms holding me close, kissing me so hard I could happily suffocate rather than come up for air.

We break the kiss and I bury my face in his neck, clinging to him like a spider monkey, realizing it's broad daylight and my dress is hiked up to fairly scandalous levels. But I don't care, breathing him in I kiss the hollow right by his collarbone, sucking in and grazing his skin with my teeth. I feel a tiny shiver run through him.

"You make it damn hard to stay in control," he grumbles teasingly, relaxing his hold enough that I loosen my legs and slide down until my feet touch the ground.

Laughing, I fix my dress, take his hand and lead him up the front steps through the impressive oak double doors, their borders hand carved with leaves and vines, complete with intimidating lions head brass knockers. Pausing in the expansive foyer, Nick looks around, taking in all the period details. The front of the mansion is literally frozen in time. Double pocket doors to the right lead to a formal dining room, to the left a parlor, all of the furniture is the original Victorian era pieces that Mrs Henderson's grandmother put in place years ago.

"I don't usually come in this way, she keeps it pretty much like a museum. At the back it's a lot less formal, I love that part," leading Nick around the stairs and down the hallway behind, the house opens up into a large kitchen on the right, living room on the left.

"Traditionally these rooms would be all walled off from each other, but at some point in the last 50 years or so, Mrs. Henderson had the walls taken down so that the living and kitchen area was all open." I pause, giving him time to look around. The space is only partially divided in the middle by a bathroom and pantry over the steps leading to the basement level.

Nick wanders into the living room, fingertips coasting over the back of the couch as he admires the large double-sided fireplace in the wall that is shared with the parlor. The far wall is covered with books. All of the woodwork is dark with age. The furniture is well worn black leather, bronze studs at the arms and around the base. The only modern touches are Mrs. Henderson's recliner in sky blue velvet facing a large flat-screen TV in the corner.

"I'm kind of surprised she's not here, parked in that recliner watching the 24-hour game show channel," I muse, walking over to the small side table beside her chair. She keeps a calendar there, and I flip it open to look at today's date.

"Oh, lunch with her son Randall, that's nice," I feel Nick behind me, hands on my waist, he rests his chin on my shoulder, his beard a delightful tickle on my neck.

"So you don't have to fight your landlady for my attention after all," Nick chuckles and brushes a kiss on the side of my neck. Releasing me, he wanders across the open expanse of polished wood floor to the kitchen. I follow him, ducking under his arm as he lifts it over my head and wraps it around me.

"This is my favorite room," I sigh. "I mean, I love the whole house, creaks and drafts and all, but this room is my favorite." I walk across the room, tracing one finger along the edge of the huge butcher block island in the center. A pot rack full of burnished copper above. On the far wall is a six burner cook top, high-end that has been made to look historical. Farmhouse sink, beautiful granite counter tops. It's a dream kitchen, and I smile every time I walk into this room.

"It looks like she's really put some work into this room," Nick walks over to the huge windows over the sink, looking out at the garden beyond, "does Mrs. Henderson like to cook too?"

I laugh, thinking about my ancient friend tooling around the kitchen with her walker, a cup of coffee and a piece of toast on the tray as she heads for her recliner.

"Oh no, she's a toast, coffee and a cigar on the back porch

kind of lady," I wave my hand around at the beautiful kitchen, "this she did for me."

Nick cocks an eyebrow at me, looking around again and I continue.

"So I had just graduated from high school, and I'd gone to community college for some credits while I figured out what to do with myself. I was living at home with my folks and all the sibs, and I was going crazy." I shake my head, remembering how crowded I felt, still sharing a room with my little sister.

"I think I already told you about how I decided on culinary school, and was looking at apartments. I needed my own space and my grandma and Mrs. Henderson are card partners, so she offered me the third floor." Nick nods, encouraging me to continue.

"I'd been here almost a year, and one day she tells me I'm going to have to be out of the house for a couple weeks, she's having some work done. I figure it's updating the pipes or electric or something, so, no problem, I stay with my parents. I came back to this kitchen." I pause, remembering.

"I asked her why in the world she did the kitchen, much less upgraded everything to restaurant level when she doesn't cook a bit, and she poked me in the chest with a bony finger and said, 'Honey, if you're going to do something you do it right. You're going to school to cook, you're going to practice on me.'" I laugh, shaking my head.

"She said she was doing the back anyway so the kitchen was an afterthought." I point between the kitchen and living area beside the giant walk-in pantry to another hallway that disappears towards the back of the house.

"So that leads to her bedroom and a sunroom with a huge solarium across the back. She was tired of climbing the stairs to the second floor so she made what used to be an office into her bedroom and added another bath." I gesture broadly at the kitchen, turning back to look at Nick.

"It was just crazy, I barely knew this old lady, and here she was believing in me. It was really cool, so I've been testing recipes on her ever since."

"It's not hard to believe in you Bree." Nick's eyes are intense as he leans on the counter listening to me and I'm immediately blushing. Nick pushes off the counter and walks over to me, his finger brushing my neck up to my cheek.

"I love this," his fingers lightly graze my cheek, sliding back through my hair until his hand is behind my neck. He gently pulls me to him as he kisses each of my flaming cheeks gently and then firmly kisses my lips, his other hand sliding around my waist. His lips part and I can't stop the moan that slips out as I lean into him, my own hands sliding around his waist to explore the muscles of his back. When we finally break apart I gasp in a breath and duck my head a little, laughing.

"I always thought it was my curse, it makes it really hard to hide what I'm feeling," I mutter, shaking my head, and then tilting it to the side with a little sigh of pleasure as his lips work their way down my neck.

"Okay not because I want to, but because my ancient landlady might walk through the door any minute, how about I rush you through the rest of the tour?" *I have a bed upstairs heh heh heh, evil laugh, twirl my mustache...stop being a dork Bree.* My voice is breathy and I *really* want him to rip my clothes off right now. With the little tiny bit of willpower I can muster, I step away from him and he laughs as I grab his hand and drag him up the servants stairs hidden in the massive pantry.

"Six bedrooms, four with attached sitting rooms, five bath-

72

rooms, four fireplaces, trust me this level is pretty cool," I say very quickly, waving my arms around like a game show girl as I pause briefly at the second floor. I pull him to the next staircase, both of us laughing at this point.

"Home sweet home," as we reach the landing I step through the door to my attic, stepping aside and turning to see Nick's reaction. He slows down and his eyes widen slightly as he reaches a hand toward me without looking, twining his fingers with mine.

The attic is mainly one huge rectangular space, dormer windows down each of the long sides and at each end a large half moon window, so there's a lot of light. The stairs are offset, entering the attic from one end, near a wall that separates off the bathroom which is positioned to have the half moon window right over the old claw foot tub. The space is broken up by brick chimneys and other support beams, with its own double sided fireplace in the center. One side of the fireplace faces my bedroom area, the other the area that I consider my living room.

"Most of the furniture was up here when I moved in, Mrs. Henderson told me to use whatever I wanted. It was all stacked up and pushed to one side under sheets to hold off the dust." Nick nods, walking around the room as he looks at some of my pictures. "Luckily I had three strong brothers who work for pizza, the extra furniture all got moved to the carriage house." I smile remembering that day, the day I'd moved into my own space.

I'd call the look I'm going for clean bohemian, it's colorful, lots of patterns and rich fabrics mixed with crisp white bedding and furniture that has a simpler style. The options stacked under the dust sheets ran heavy into jewel tones and velvet, once again making me question if this place took a little tour as a bordello. There was a mix of some cool side chairs and tables that were more ornate as well as a lot of furniture that was either bought later or was just simple because it was for the servants, I don't know much about furniture. Whatever the case, the ornate pieces are a dark mahogany, and the simple pieces are a beautiful light maple. I show all of this to Nick as we slowly walk from one end to the other and he looks out the large window at the end of the bedroom side.

"So after I picked out all the pieces I wanted to use, and brought in my own bed, the rest of the furniture went up to the second floor of the carriage house." I point out the window as we look over the grounds. Along with the carriage house, there is a greenhouse, an outbuilding where the mower and other equipment is stored, and further back by the trees, a caretakers cottage.

"The Nelsons live there," I tell him, indicating the cottage. "They've basically retired and they spend a lot of time visiting all their grandkids. Barnaby keeps the cars in top shape and manages the guys that tend the grounds." I shrug, "Louise comes in once a month and gives the house a good cleaning top to bottom, and she'll check in on Mrs. H. if I'm not around. They're really nice, I'm pretty sure they've been with her for years and years."

I trail off, glancing at Nick. I wonder what he thinks of where I live. I know he grew up in the full silver spoon, white glove situation, so maybe this is too far out of his norm. I hope he sees the glow of the old wood, the rich history. I love this place.

He's quiet, taking it all in, and suddenly I'm not sure I should have brought him up here. Maybe I'm just a mouse in the attic and this is how he'll realize that I'm not enough for him, that we're just too different. *Where the crap did that come from? He likes me, he told me...he showed me.* A rush of heat shoots straight from my chest to my head, flooding my cheeks, yeah, he showed me.

*But what if he's not sure now? In the heat of last night it was easy, but maybe today is different...*I mentally duct tape my inner voice's mouth shut, because I don't know what her damn problem is today, and give his hand a little squeeze. Nick jumps, tearing his gaze away from the view outside and smiles down at me.

"I was just thinking you're really lucky," he pauses and I let out a little grunt of disbelief.

"No, really," his eyes crinkle just a tiny bit at the corners as his smile widens. "I grew up in a big house like this, but all the history had been modernized right out of every room. My parents liked white and clean and minimalist. It was beautiful in a way, but it always felt pretty sterile. My father sold it when my mother died. I often miss her, but I don't miss the house."

Dropping my hand he circles an arm around my shoulders, pulling me in tight to his side. I'm not sure what I should say, and he must not want me to be drawn into the somber mood he accidentally created because he leans down and rumbles right in my ear.

"Any house in the world would be perfect if I opened the door and found you." *SWOON SWOON SWOON, oh hello Inner Voice, glad to see you put your romantic pants back on!* My eyes slide shut as I give a pleased little sigh and let his voice vibrate straight to my heart.

Don't Piss Off a Rich Man

Nick

I am about to very un-subtly grab Bree and take advantage of the bed we are standing next to when my phone pings. Pulling it out of my pocket to silence it, I see Sanford's name on the text and swipe it open instead.

> SW: Get to my office asap.
> Me: why, what happened
> SW: Just get here, we've got a problem.

Now I'm concerned, Sanford doesn't often text, preferring just to make the phone call, so he must be with people. Bree notices and leans to see the screen.

"Well that doesn't sound good, what's up?" She gives me a

squeeze and I lean down to give her a kiss.

"No idea, but I'm going to have to go, William's doesn't usually run up against problems he can't handle without me." Kissing her lips again and then dropping another kiss on her hair, I force my arms to let go of her and start to walk to the stairs. Glancing back, I see her following me, a worried crease between her eyes.

"Hope this doesn't have anything to do with the creampuff incident," she mutters with a nervous smile. I laugh and turn back to hug her one more time *well, now that you mention it, maybe.*

"I'm sure it doesn't, I'll call you tonight." We walk down the stairs and out to my jeep, she gives me a kiss and then a wave from the porch as I drive down the lane.

Thirty minutes later I'm walking into Sanford's office. He's at his desk working, when I arrive, his face stern.

"Did you break up with Veronica in a fairly confrontational fashion last night Nick?" *Shit.*

"Well breakup is too strong a word since we weren't ever really in a committed relationship, but yes, it would be safe to say that I ended things with Veronica last night. Tell me why that matters Williams." I grumble, dropping into a chair across from him.

"It matters because John Rockford owns 1438 Washington Avenue, Nick." He throws the papers in his hand on the desk in front of him and scrubs a hand over his closely cropped silver hair. I feel a weight drop into my stomach.

"Veronica's father owns the building that houses my gallery, is that what you mean Williams? How did I not know that vital piece of information!" I realize I'm almost shouting and I pause, visibly pulling myself together.

"Sorry, but how did you find out, what does that mean?"

"It means that I was paid a visit by one of his attorneys this afternoon. He informed me that by eight o'clock Monday morning, your gallery will be moving into storage while we look for a new space to lease," Williams responds crisply, nodding at my apology. "One of his smaller holding companies is actually the name on the title of many of these buildings downtown. He's kept that very private information until now. It explains why we've never found a building we could just buy outright. Finding a new place will not be easy," Williams huffs in annoyance.

"Is there a way to fight this? I mean they can't just say 'get out' and give me a day to clear out, isn't there a process?" I need a direction for my anger, I need an outlet. I need to fix this. *Right. Fucking. Now.*

"I haven't told you the worst part yet, Nick." Williams laces his fingers together, not making eye contact.

"The reason you have until Monday morning is because if you don't get out he's going to have Breanna arrested for assault. I don't even know why she was with you at the gallery, I could have hired extra help, but obviously that girl is fired. To put us in the position of such terrible publicity for the gallery, that little-" he cuts off staring at me as I growl a curse and slap my palms on the top of his desk, the noise startling us both.

"Bree wasn't there as help, she was there with me, as in *with me.*" I ignore Williams' narrowed eyes as his mouth opens to interrupt, "She didn't lay a finger on Veronica, even though Veronica was laying on the queen bitch routine hard last night. Bree flicked a tray of cream puffs at her and most of them stuck to her ass," remembering that moment last night, I want to laugh again, but I don't think Williams would see the humor.

I'm wrong.

Williams' mouth drops open in astonishment and then he's laughing. Really laughing. Laughing so hard he tears up. When he finally starts to slow down, he pulls a silk handkerchief out of his suit pocket and mops his face, still chuckling.

"Cream puffs all over her ass…the comeuppance of a tabloid socialite," he chortles, shaking his head, "Oh I am sorry I missed that. That damn lawyer made it sound like unprovoked fisticuffs resulting in a battered and bruised Veronica, crawling home. What an ass." He tucks the handkerchief away and focuses on me again, taking in the look of open astonishment on my face. "Why are you looking at me like that?"

I'm struggling to find the words, but I finally stutter, "I thought you set me up with Veronica, I thought you wanted me to be with her?!"

"God no," Williams scoffed. "Veronica was an acquaintance of Laurel's and she got a look at you at that charity gala Rockford threw a few months back. She badgered Laurel until Laurel caved and asked me if I could arrange an introduction. I thought you would politely give her the brush off, I never dreamed you'd actually date the woman," he pauses, looking at me seriously. "So out of curiosity, why did you?"

I shift and look away, suddenly uncomfortable. In many ways, Sanford Williams has taken on the role of a father figure in my life since my father's death. However, that role has largely been in keeping me from making errors in my business decisions and providing a family atmosphere for me during the holidays. We don't talk women. *Clearly if I thought he would want me to be with a brat like Veronica. It never occurred to me to question that match, I'm an idiot.*

Williams, sensing my discomfort, gives me a moment while

he stands and crosses the room to his liquor cabinet. Pouring us each two fingers of whiskey he hands one to me and sits back in his chair, waiting quietly.

"I'm guessing you've noticed I don't do relationships very well," I grimace at the glass in my hands, thinking back on the women I've been with over the past few years. Williams doesn't reply, just takes another swallow of whiskey and waits for me to continue.

"I think I'm always wondering what I should be looking for," I pause, trying to find better words. "More than that, I always wonder what I can give a woman. I mean I know I'm good-looking, have money, I get it. But past that, what is a woman going to want from me?" I knock back the whiskey in a big gulp and set the glass down on the table beside me. Standing, I walk to the window looking outside but seeing nothing.

"I think I'm afraid a woman will want something I can't or won't want to give. I date women like Veronica because all they want is the outside package, they don't want anything deeper." Turning back to Williams, I hesitate before adding, "Bree is different."

"In what way?" Williams continues to watch me, his eyes unreadable.

"I want her to want everything from me," I say quietly, turning back to the window. "I don't know how it happened but I want to give that woman the air that I breathe, the sun on my face, everything I am, she could ask for it all, and it would be hers..." my voice has gone rough with emotion, "...and I want her to be mine." *I'm in love. I didn't even see it coming, but there it is, love.*

After a few moments, Williams clears his throat gently.

"Your father felt like that about your mother you know," he

says quietly. I nod, not trusting myself to speak.

"He used to call her his night," Williams continues, "I asked him why once, and he said it was something his father had told him when he was first out on his own." I nod again, rubbing a hand across my chest unconsciously.

"Your grandfather, and then your father, believed that any good woman could fill a man's days. Any good woman could tend a home, raise a child, keep a man happy. Clearly it was a different time." He pauses again, smiling and swirling the whiskey left in his glass thoughtfully.

"He said he knew she was the one when he not only wanted to spend his days with her but every last one of his nights as well." Williams drains the rest of his whiskey, "Maybe you've found your night Nick."

An Unexpected Visitor

Nick

*A*fter a few moments Williams turns the conversation to the pressing issue of moving the gallery and I'm relieved. I need time to think about everything he said. I heard my father call my mother his night many times when I was a child, he explained what it meant on my eighteenth birthday. At the time I had smiled at the sentiment but I hadn't understood the depth of feeling he was trying to convey. I just wasn't equipped to understand love at 18.

Leaving Williams busy making calls and arranging to have everything safely stored temporarily, I head for my loft, put in a hard workout and shower. As I towel off I hear the intercom buzzing for the lobby door. Not even bothering to check the camera, I push the button and buzz Bree up, throwing on some clothes as I hear the door to the loft open. Walking out to greet her, the hello dies on my lips.

It's Veronica.

"I got the message, Williams is emptying the gallery as we speak." I grit out, angrily.

"I'm sorry!" Veronica snaps, her usual cool, spoiled demeanor gone. "My driver told my father a highly embellished version of my trip home, I was upset, I didn't mean for things to go this far," she looks down at her hands, nervous.

"I wasn't sure you'd take my call, so I thought I would just come and tell you in person. I can't do anything about him kicking you out of the gallery, but nothing is going to happen to Bree. I refused to talk to the police and I'm not going to press any charges," she snorts delicately.

"What the hell would I tell them anyway? That I was a bitch and someone threw a bunch of desserts at me?" Veronica rolls her eyes, some of her usual confidence returning.

"She's got fire, I'll give her that," Veronica shrugs, "I was long overdue for a wake-up call, it's not often someone gives me one. Hell, in another life we probably would have been friends," with a little laugh she walks to the door, opens it and then turns back to me.

"I hope she's what you're looking for, Nick. I'm sorry we didn't work, I'm not sure I know what I'm looking for either," she smiles and blows me a little kiss as she walks out the door.

Out of the Frying Pan

Nick

*S*tanding there for a moment, I shake my head and try to make sense of the last ten minutes. I still have to move the gallery, but Bree is in the clear. I shoot a text to Williams to update him on this turn of events and notice that I've missed a call and there's a voicemail. It's Bree. She sounds like she's walking fast, kind of breathless, upset.

"Nick, there's been an accident," my heart stops until she continues, "Mrs. Henderson fell leaving the restaurant with Randall and they're doing x-rays now but Randall says they're pretty sure her leg is broken and something is wrong with her shoulder…" she stops to catch her breath and I can hear her choking back a small sob. "I don't know how she's doing, she's pretty old and it was a bad fall…her son is a wreck. I'm going to stay with him at the hospital, there isn't any other family, I'll call you when I can. I, um, well that's it, I hope everything is okay on your end. Bye." She disconnects.

I call her and it goes straight to voicemail. I disconnect and my phone pings.

> Bree: Hey sorry Dr is in here
> Me: Which hospital?
> Bree: St Vincents
> Me: I'm coming

Tossing my phone and a few other things in a backpack in case it's a long night, I'm on the road in minutes. The sterile antiseptic smell hits me in the face as I walk in the doors, and as I turn down the hall, Bree is there. She's leaning on the wall next to the door to Mrs. Henderson's room, face in her hands, shoulders shaking. I gather her in my arms and she wraps her arms around my waist tight, crying into the front of my shirt.

"What's happened? What can I do?" I can't stand to see her hurting.

"She's out of surgery, but they think she's bleeding some-where inside, and they can't get it stopped," Bree hiccups quietly, her forehead on my chest. "She's awake a little bit of the time, and I just couldn't hold it in anymore, the doctor said the biggest worry is a stroke, they're doing what they can, giving her transfusions and stuff." Bree leans back and gives me a watery smile. "When she was awake I told her about you, she told me I had to share," Bree gives a little laugh that ends as a sob and I pull her close again, mumbling nonsense comfort words and rubbing her back.

The door next to Bree opens, and a man who looks to be

in his early 70s comes out shutting the door quietly behind him. Silver hair, wire framed glasses, he offers Bree a tired smile. She conjures up a smile of her own and introduces me to Randall.

"Nice to meet you, wish it were for a happier reason," Randall says quietly, shaking my hand. "Mother is sleeping, I'm going to go down to the cafeteria and see if I can get my hands on a sandwich and a coffee. Can you two sit with her until I get back? I wouldn't want her to wake up alone." We nod and he heads for the elevator.

Walking into her room, Mrs. Henderson is tiny. I would be surprised if she was five feet tall, a cloud of silvery white hair frames her face on the pillow. She is very pale, one leg wrapped to the knee, her arm is in a sling with pillows positioned to keep it from moving as she sleeps.

Bree walks up to the bedside and smooths her hair and she stirs, opening bright blue eyes.

"Hey pumpkin, you're still here? It has to be getting late and *helloooooo* brown eyes," she catches sight of me and gives a weak little cackle as Bree lets loose a startled giggle, glancing at me. Smiling, I take the older woman's tiny hand and gently kiss a knuckle.

"At your service Mrs. Henderson," I say quietly, smiling.

"Oh my goodness, I thought I was too old but I might just have a hot flash, you've got a live one here pumpkin," Mrs. Henderson laughs weakly, reaching her other hand out to pat Bree's cheek gently. She turns back to me and those blue eyes sharpen, piercing and stern.

"Are you going to take good care of my girl? She deserves the best, and I fully intend to haunt anyone who doesn't treat her right." It is easy to picture the woman she must have been in her youth, proud and strong, her tone brooks no nonsense. I nod solemnly.

"I'm hers if she'll have me Mrs. Henderson." I reply, glancing at Bree just in time to catch that beautiful blush creeping up her neck to color her cheeks. Mrs. Henderson nods as if that settles everything and squeezes my hand once hard before letting go. She pats Bree's cheek again and whispers, "he's a keeper honey," before going back to sleep.

She never opens her eyes again. At some point in the night, while Bree, Randall and I are asleep in chairs near her bed, Mrs. Henderson quietly takes her last breath. The funeral is a small, quiet affair. Randall was Mrs. Henderson's only son, and he never married. By the time you're 98 years old, I guess it's safe to say that most of your friends are waiting on the other side.

Damn, This is Perfect

Bree

Nick took me to the house to gather some things and then quietly moved me into his loft. I was grateful, it would have been hard to stay in that big old house alone right away. I'm not sure what's going to happen to the house now that Mrs. H. is gone, I supposed Randall will either move into it or sell it.

Nick has been really busy, he told me he had planned to move into a new gallery space for better lighting and more room, but somehow the timeline got moved up drastically. He makes up for the time I don't see him during the day by consuming my nights.

It's been two weeks of amazing nights, *and some early mornings,* learning what the other likes, *really likes.* Just thinking about the things that man does to my body makes my underpants burst into flames. I glance at the clock, realizing I've been brushing my teeth for more than five minutes while I daydream about him.

As I bend over to spit and rinse in the sink, I hear him pad into the bathroom barefoot. He lets out a low groan and his strong hands are on my hips. He leans in to grind against my ass and I brace my hands on the edge of the counter and look over my shoulder at him, smiling.

He leans forward and cups my chin with one hand, kissing me hard, still pressed against my ass. When we break the kiss, he trails his lips down my neck and gently grazes his teeth over my shoulder. I feel his thumbs hook into either side of my panties and push them off my hips to fall to the floor.

Our eyes lock in the mirror as he shifts his hips back and I moan and arch my back, giving him better access. With a deep groan he grabs my hips and buries himself in my heat with one deep stroke, forcing another moan from my lips as my eyes slide shut.

His hands slide up to my waist. I'm wearing a small lace tank top, and his fingers gather it and shove it up, his hands cupping my tits as he pumps in and out of me slowly.

"Look at me," he rumbles, setting his teeth lightly to my shoulder, continuing his rhythm, as my eyes fly open and find his in the mirror. I move my hands from the counter to the mirror, spread my feet a tiny bit wider and arch so that he hits that spot deep inside.

"I want to watch you," he rasps out, voice rough. I smile at him in the mirror, my right hand sliding down my body. With a gasp his hands squeeze tight and he pumps faster. His eyes are full of heat as he stares into mine in the mirror. I watch his gaze move down my body as I stroke myself while he watches, and I start to lose control. Matching his rhythm, I feel him shortening his strokes, building up to his own release. I hover on that sweet edge as long as I can before I have to throw my head back on his shoulder.

"Harder Nick, yes, oh-oh yes!" My nipples tighten and my core clenches, his hands grip my hips and he pumps hard and fast. I scream my pleasure and his low cries join mine as we spasm together. As we ride out the aftershocks, every little movement bringing a shiver, he leans against me, one strong arm sliding around my waist while his other hand braces on the counter to hold us up. He's still buried inside my body, and I don't want to move.

I feel his lips on my neck, laying gentle kisses down to my shoulder. His eyes meet mine and he sighs, resting his chin on my shoulder.

"I love you, Bree," he murmurs. My eyes widen and I can't stop the smile on my lips or the blush blooming on my cheeks. He smiles and kisses my cheek as I reach a hand back sliding it up his neck. My fingers knot in his hair as I turn and capture his lips with mine.

"I love you, Nick," I gasp when we come up for air, my hands on his face, looking into his eyes. I'm home, his answering smile is everything and he doesn't look away as he reaches back and turns on the shower. Taking my hand he pulls me into the warm water.

Nick's Desk? Check.

Bree

I sleep in the next morning because, well, no commute. *I swear I am a laugh a minute.* Splashing some water on my face and brushing my teeth, I pull on Nick's robe and walk down the hall to his office.

He's on the phone, but he motions me in, smiling. I lean my butt on the edge of his desk and the hand that he's not using to hold his phone slides inside the robe as he strokes up and down my thigh. He wraps up the call and pulls me into his lap, kissing me on the lips before ducking his head to plant another kiss between my boobs peeking out of the V in the robe.

"I have to go out of town for a few days," he says, muffled

because his face is still between my boobs, his beard tickling me. I giggle and squirm a little, and he looks up smiling.

"I'd like to take you with me," he says, serious now. *Yes, yes-yes-yes anywhere, anytime, wait, nooooo not right now, dammit.*

"Nick I wish I could, but Clary graduates this weekend, my mom is counting on me to take care of all the food and about a billion cupcakes for her party on Saturday," his face falls, but he keeps smiling. "I really would like to go," I continue earnestly, I reach for his face, looking in his eyes. "When are you leaving? Will you be able to be back for the party? I was hoping you could…maybe meet my family," I stutter through the last part, nervous.

His eyes widen, and he leans in for a kiss.

"If I leave tonight I should be able to be back in time," he smiles, "throwing me to the wolves huh?" I punch him playfully in the shoulder.

"Naw, that would be if I left you alone with Margo," I laugh, starting to stand up, but he keeps hold of my waist, kissing between my boobs again.

"If I have to leave tonight, I'll need something to dream about while I'm gone," he rumbles, muffled by my tits as he lifts me up to sit on the desk in front of him. He unties the belt of the robe and kisses his way down my belly, then kisses the inside of each of my thighs. Goosebumps erupt everywhere he touches and his strong hands lay me back on his desk. He spreads my legs, puts one over each of his shoulders and makes me forget my own name. *Twice.*

This Will Hold Me Over

Nick

I will never get tired of Bree screaming my name. She's panting as she lays back on the desk, and I have never been so hard in my life. I can taste her on my lips. I lay kisses on the insides of her thighs and hear a shaky laugh.

"I swear if you do me again I will explode into pieces so small they'll need dental records," she gasps. "I'm not having much luck convincing any of my muscles to move right now, and I'd really like to take advantage of you." She pauses, getting her breath under control, "Could you do me a favor and get naked and come around to the other side of your desk?"

Laughing, I stand, making a noticeable tent in the track pants I'm wearing. Pulling my t-shirt over my head, I drop it on the floor, walking around the desk. The look she is giving me is pure sex as she scoots up, dropping her head partly over the edge of the desk, opening her lips. She licks them and I step closer with a groan. Her lips and her heat and the noises she makes, Bree's perfect body writhing on my desk grants every wish I've ever made.

* * *

Collapsing into my desk chair, she giggles as I pull her into my lap, kissing the side of my neck before she shifts to stand. Gathering the robe around her she gives me an impish grin.

"Now we both have something to dream about while you're gone," she says with a wink as she saunters down the hall.

I fucking love this woman.

It's the Little Things

Bree

My mother is doing a fantastic job keeping me busy with my mind off missing Nick during the day, but the nights are long without his heat in the bed. I miss his voice and his hands on my body.

My mother and Margo have tag-teamed me incessantly for details about Nick. I thank the stars for all those meals we ate together over the past year, because I even surprise myself sometimes at the little details I've picked up.

His favorite color is green, he speaks fluent French, his birthday is in November. He cuts all that thick dark hair off every other year and donates it to charity. Pineapple makes him gag. *Found that one out the hard way.* His tattoo is Latin... *nox inveniat,* we were laying in bed one night and I was tracing the letters curling across his ribs and I asked him what it meant.

"It's a reminder of something my father told me once," he'd said simply, kissing my forehead.

"Earth to Bree," my mother's voice is teasing as she bumps her shoulder into mine, making me jump as I realize I'm standing in her kitchen, I've stopped cooking and I have a silly smile on my face. Face flaming I continue stirring the mixture for those silly little buttercream mints because Mom had to go *traditional.* She's been hunting for all the punchbowl cups too, I don't have the heart to tell her the boys broke four of them one time when I was babysitting. *Translation, she'd be mad and I'm a coward.*

My mom sucks in a breath and I know she's going to launch into round 36 of interrogation about Nick when my phone rings. She takes the spoon out of my hand and waves me off.

"Go ahead, I'll finish this," she smiles.

Glancing at the screen, the call is from Randall Henderson. I answer, hoping he's not going to tell me I have to move out this weekend.

"Hi Randall, how are you?"

"Bree, I'm good, still getting things settled," he says warmly. "Say I just wanted to call and let you know the reading of Mom's will is tomorrow morning at ten. If you could be there, that'd be great, I know she remembered you when she was making some changes to it a couple years ago."

"Really?…I'm surprised…I mean I helped her out and I loved her like my favorite grumpy grandma, but I wasn't expecting her to put me in her *will.*" I see my mom's ears perk up as she turns to me with curiosity burning in her eyes.

"…favorite grumpy grandma," Randall bursts out laughing, "Oh she would have loved that. Don't underestimate what you meant to her Bree, her exact words to me in the hospital before you arrived were, 'Randall, you watch this girl, she's going to have a great life if she keeps her head out of her ass.'"

Now we're both laughing and maybe crying a little because we miss that gruff old lady with a heart of gold, and I manage to tell him that I'll be there and end the call.

I brace myself and wander back out to the kitchen, stalling off my mom's questions by holding up one hand.

"Before you ask, yes, apparently Mrs. Henderson left me something in her will. No, I don't know what it is, probably her second favorite gravy bowl. I'll find out tomorrow morning," Pushing everything else out of my head for the moment, I head for the fridge to gather ingredients for the next appetizer I want to have ready ahead of time. If I'm going to this will reading tomorrow morning, it's time to get busy finishing up the food.

Mrs Henderson's Gift

Bree

*T*he reading of Mrs. Henderson's will is simple, it's over in less than 20 minutes. Signing papers takes a little longer. I'm in a state of shock, and I insist that Randall and I step into a private room to talk for a moment.

"Randall, I had no idea she was going to do this, if you want me to I will sign it over to you-," I burst out, wringing my hands.

"Don't you dare, kiddo," he smiles. "I'm well taken care of, she left me more than I'll ever need and I don't have children of my own to leave anything to when I'm gone. She did the right thing." He gives me a wink. "If you're going to fill it up, you and that man of yours better get busy making some babies."

He laughs even harder as I blush and ushers me back into the lawyer's office.

Walking through the front door of my parent's home an hour later, I kick off my shoes on the entry rug and head into the living room, throwing myself on the couch. My mother hears me and comes bustling out of the kitchen.

"Well?" Patience is not a virtue my mother possesses. "What happened? Did she have a lot? Living in that big rickety house I always thought she was probably scraping by on social security checks, but you said she did that big kitchen remodel so she must have had some money squirreled awa-," I cut in on my mother's rapid fire questioning.

"She left everything to Randall and I, Mom. There was kind of a lot," *Massive understatement, colossal in fact.* Unsure of how to explain what exactly Mrs. Henderson did for me, all of a sudden I'm crying.

"She left Randall a big chunk of money, several million dollars...some sentimental things, and whatever he wants from the house," I manage to blurt out through my tears, barely registering my mother's quiet, "oh my god" as she stares at me.

"She left me...everything else," I blubber, and suddenly I can't sit still. I bounce off the couch, pacing to the window and back as my mother tries to form a question.

"All of it Mom, a lot of money, *more than 10 million dollars,* the house, the land...everything." I finish on a whisper. My mother isn't even trying to talk anymore, she's sunk into the spot on the couch that I vacated, staring at me.

We stare at each other for several long moments before she comes off the couch like she was shot out of a cannon, and she's hugging me and we're both crying. Somehow I manage to tell her all the details and about the talk I had with Randall.

There was also a lot of talk about different trusts and things that were set up so that I don't lose most of the money as taxes, but I'll figure all that out later.

Eventually we're both calm, and we start getting dinner ready. The big graduation party is tomorrow afternoon, but all my siblings, Margo, and a few other aunts and uncles will be over tonight for dinner. Before I throw myself into cooking, my mother stops me and puts her hands on my shoulders, looking at me intently.

"I want you to understand that money is yours," she says firmly, "ah-ah-ah," she tuts as I open my mouth to protest, "let me finish. We are fine, we are happy, and we have everything we need. We raised five kind, beautiful, intelligent children and we have each other and our health. There is nothing else I want," she finishes simply, squeezing my shoulders and giving a brisk, 'that's settled' nod of her head. I don't even try to argue, I just know I'll have to be creative. Smiling, I step up to the counter and start chopping vegetables.

Family starts to arrive, and an hour later the house is loud and boisterous, and I'm squawking at my brothers.

"Fingers out of that pot! Get the hell out of the kitchen," brandishing a wooden spoon and laughing I chase them out only to turn around and find Clary sliding the lid back over the mints, a guilty smile on her face.

"You twerp, those are for tomorrow! Be warned, I will never be too old to tattle to Mom on ANY of you!" She scuttles out of the kitchen, laughing as my Mom herds everyone to the table. The table has been extended to full capacity, and it takes up the dining room straight through a large archway to the living room, with a card table tacked on the end so that we can all sit together.

The group is silent for 25 seconds while my dad says grace, and then it's game on. Every dish of food on the table is passed around, plates are piled high, and the usual complaints from my Uncle Ron about forgetting to wear his 'fat pants' commence. In the midst of the chaos, I register the doorbell ringing. Hopping up, I toss my napkin on my chair and head for the front door, mentally doing a headcount to see who's not at the table yet. My mom hears the bell as well and follows me out to the entryway at the far end of the living room.

"I got back to town early," Nick smiles as I gasp in surprise, he pulls me into a one-armed hug, laying a kiss on the top of my head as he hands me the bottle of wine in his hand. Releasing me, he smiles at my mother who is hovering at my shoulder and hands her the bundle of flowers he was holding in his other hand. Snapping out of it, I introduce them.

"Brace yourself," I mutter for his ears alone as my mother takes the flowers exclaiming about what a gentleman I've found. Then she grabs his hand, dragging him to the table for introductions, hissing at my dad to get another chair.

"This one is vacant," Margo trills, quickly shoving Clary out of the chair next to her with a quick glare to find another seat. *Oh boy...I may need to accidentally-on-purpose dump that bottle of wine on my lap so I have to go home.*

Dinner in the Burbs

Nick

I have never been to a family dinner like this in my life. Bree's family is great. I'm wedged between Margo and Clary, they pepper me with questions, Bree's mother, Susan, is running around the table piling a plate high. Bree's brothers are across the table keeping a close eye on me. Bree sits further down the table looking like she's ready to dump a bottle of wine in her lap so she can drag me out of here before Margo tells me any more about the beautiful spring wedding she attended.

I give Bree a quick wink as I dig into the food and smile at Clary who blushes just like her big sister. She's a sweet kid, and she's done well in school, tells me she's going to college in the fall to study music and she's got a full ride scholarship.

Congratulating her, I talk with Margo about what Bree was like as a kid, Bree's face is flaming as Margo regales our end of the table with stories. They all start with, "Do you remember that time that Bree...?" and usually end up with Bree naked in the front yard or covered in some combination of mud, food and glitter.

Pushing back from the table, begging Susan not to fill my plate with anymore food, I stand up to stretch, and Bree's dad, Bill, taps my arm, motioning for me to follow him to the den. He laughs lightly as he pours me a drink and hands it to me, raising his in a quick salute as we settle into comfy leather chairs.

"Bree's never brought anyone home before," Bill says gravely, eyeing me over the top of his glass. "Not since high school dances and such...you must be someone special." He pauses, waiting for me to speak.

"I hope so, Bill, I know your daughter is special to me." I respond, relieved when he nods and takes another sip of his drink. We talk a little longer, and then we're joined by Bree's brothers and Uncle Ron. The conversation turns to Friday's game and the time passes easily, eventually Bree and her mother wander in and Bree perches on the arm of my chair. I slide an arm around her waist and she leans down to whisper in my ear.

"Take me home, Nick." A tingle runs right down my spine as her breath hits my ear and it's all I can do not to just pick her up and walk out the door. We begin our goodbyes, and I exchange a few more words with her father as she hugs her mom and sister. She turns back as Bill and I shake hands and looks at me, curious.

"Well that was formal, did you just sell him a painting?" She jokes as we head out the door. Looping an arm around her shoulders, I pull her in close, kissing her temple as we walk to my car.

"Yep, one for every room of the house," I grin, she gives me a little elbow to the ribs and I pinch her lightly on the ass. She squeals and pulls away laughing as we get in the car. Before I back the car out of the driveway, I lean over and kiss her.

"I missed you." I murmur as I pull back, and she smiles and laces her fingers through mine, "I'm glad I came back early, your family is great."

"Oh yeah, great…was it the naked nudie stories or the man talk in the den that sold you on me?" She laughs, shaking her head. Giving her hand a gentle squeeze, I laugh with her.

"All of it, in fact I'd like you to re-enact all those 'naked nudie' stories in full detail," we're both laughing now, and finally she sighs and we ride in silence for a while.

"So I didn't get to ask how your trip went," she turns to look at me. I sigh and shake my head,

"It was a bust, the artist I went to meet was a diva, and I'm looking a little farther afield for gallery locations. I don't want to move, but I'm not finding the space I need in the downtown locations. *Also Rockford owns most of it.*

"Move?" Her eyes widen, "I hope you don't have to either, what are you looking for exactly?"

"I'd just like to find something a little different, a wide open space that maybe even connects to an outdoor space. I had high hopes for a place downtown that had an atrium in the center, but no luck." I squeeze her hand again, "Don't worry, Love, if I had to move I'd find a way to convince you to come with me." I lift her hand up to mine and lay a kiss across her knuckles.

"That wouldn't be hard," she sighs contentedly, "believe me if I said no, my mom and Margo would be there to hog-tie me and throw me in your trunk, they love you."

"How about you, did you have a good day?" I've spoken to her every night, so I know she was mostly busy helping prep for the graduation party, but she had mentioned having to meet Randall Henderson at a lawyer's office this morning. She doesn't respond and when I look at her in the dim light of the car, she's fallen asleep.

Party in the Burbs

Bree

The next morning we are at my parent's house bright and early. Nick is being a great sport, helping my dad and brothers set up a large tent in the backyard and then they all begin a game of washers, avoiding my mother. I can tell Nick's never played before, but to my father's delight as his partner, he's a ringer. *Shocker, he's never played a game that involves throwing two-inch washers at a coffee can sitting in a wooden box...*I laugh to myself picturing what his family parties might have looked like. It sounds like his childhood was mostly uber-formal.

Arguing good-naturedly over the points, Nick sees me watching and raises his beer in a quick toast in my direction, I smile and give him a quick finger wave, heading back in to help my mom. I find her in the kitchen, watching the guys play through the window as she washes a few last bowls that wouldn't fit in the dishwasher.

"He seems like a good guy, he sure gets along with your dad and the boys," Mom nods out the window and looks at me.

"Yeah, he's great," I smile and start drying the bowls and stacking them on a pantry shelf.

"He had a good talk with your dad last night," Mom continues, still watching me.

"That's good, I hope Dad didn't pour Nick any of that really crap whiskey Uncle Ron gives him every Christmas," we laugh together, watching the game as we finish the dishes. After a few minutes, my mom clears her throat quietly, wiping her hands on a towel.

"Have you told him about your inheritance?"

"No, not yet, I fell asleep in the car on the way home, and I figured with the party today I'd wait, he's had a lot on his mind with his gallery," I sigh, thinking, I've been mulling over what I could do to help him, but I'm not ready to talk about that yet.

"Well that's probably smart," she chuckles, "You know he's not seeing you for your money at least."

"Mom!" I dissolve into giggles, "I guess when he does find out he'll know I'm not seeing him for his money either."

The game outside is ending, my father is shaking Nick's hand and claps him on the back as they head for the garage to grab another beer. Guests are starting to arrive and soon I'm caught up in the whirlwind of keeping the tables loaded with food so that my mom can talk to all the guests.

The party is a success, eventually my mom makes my dad mingle with her, talking to friends and family, and Nick comes into the kitchen. Walking up behind me as I load a tray of cupcakes, he slides his arms around my waist and hugs me, laying a kiss on the side of my neck. My eyes slide closed for a minute and I lean back into him, smiling.

"Thank you for being so great with my family," I murmur as we sway in time with the music filtering in from the party in the backyard.

"They make it very easy," he rumbles quietly, laying another kiss on my neck. Letting go of my waist, he helps me load the trays and carries one while I follow with the other out to the food tables. Setting them down and surveying the spread, everything looks great. My dad has a tiki torch and twinkle light paradise set up in the backyard, people are laughing and dancing and having fun.

Lacing my fingers through Nick's, I pull him towards the door that leads into the garage. Several people are in there refilling drinks, and we smile and nod as I lead him to the door that opens out to the front yard. At the side of the house there's a small porch that's walled in by shrubs, and the street lights don't reach that far. *Secret make out spot from high school. Still works.*

I pull Nick up to the porch and turn to him, sliding my arms around his waist, tilting my face up to meet him for a kiss. His lips crash into mine and his hands slide up my back and tangle in my hair. He backs me up to the wall of the house and leans into me with a low groan. Parting my lips I feel the flick of his tongue and his teeth graze my lower lip as he sucks it in, sending a jolt straight to my clit.

One of his hands slides back down my back to cup my ass before sliding lower and lifting my leg up to wrap around his hip. His cock is cradled against my center, and he grinds into me slowly, kissing his way across my jaw and down my neck. Finding the skin over my collarbone, he sucks in, lightly marking me as I find the hem of his shirt and slide my hands under, exploring the muscles of his back.

The door to the garage opens and we freeze as several people walk out, talking and laughing as they head to their cars, just on the other side of the bushes hiding us from sight. Sliding his hand back up my ass to my back, Nick lets my leg lower to the ground, and we stand together, foreheads touching, no sound but our ragged breathing and pounding hearts. I feel him smile as he kisses me, and then he steps back, lacing his fingers through mine.

"So, just to be clear," he coughs lightly, "It would probably undo all the points I've earned with your parents if they found us having sex on their porch?"

"Most definitely." Giggling I lean forward, kissing his lips lightly, "But maybe you could give me a hickey to hide from my mom, just to commemorate me bringing you to my old high school make-out spot."

"Oh that can be arranged," he rumbles, smiling evilly and pulling me close as I squeal and he nuzzles my neck. His fingers slide the neck of my shirt down, giving him access, and my gasp turns into a soft moan of pleasure as his lips find the upper curve of my breast. His lips part and he sucks in hard, I feel just a hint of his teeth and my panties are instantly soaked. He stops sucking and kisses the mark he left before letting my shirt slide back up to cover it.

"That one can be our secret," his eyes are midnight shadows as they meet mine and I shiver. *Fuuuck, I want him so bad.* I swear he can read my mind because he smiles and kisses me lightly.

"Later," he promises, taking my hand and leading me back

to the party.

Behind the Ink

Nick

The party is winding down, and Bree's mother shoos us out the door with hugs and smiles.

"You kids go on, the boys will help me," turning her head she hollers toward the backyard, "OH SHUT IT, YOU'RE HELPING," before turning back to us with a grin. "We've got it all taken care of honey, you've been on your feet all day." Giving Bree another squeeze, she disappears back into the house barking orders at Bree's brothers.

"She must *realllllllly* like you," Bree laughs, reaching up and tugging lightly on my beard, "This face just got us out of clean up duty! Unprecedented!"

"Aw shucks, ma'am," I duck my head and smile as she laughs even harder. Leaning down, it's my turn to laugh at her startled squawk as I toss her over my shoulder and fireman carry her to my jeep. Running my fingers down the cleft of her ass I find the hem of her skirt. Reaching under, I skim over the lace triangle covering her pussy, smiling as I hear her gasp with pleasure, wiggling her butt for more attention. Carefully dumping her in the seat and leaning in for a kiss, I stare into her eyes for a moment and her breath quickens.

"I love you," I say quietly, kissing her gently before shutting her door and walking around the jeep to drive us home.

We're quiet during the drive, enjoying the silence after the chaos of the party. I'm idly stroking her leg, so smooth, and she's got her eyes closed, a small smile on her face. Walking into the loft, I smile in anticipation. I've been thinking about this moment all day.

"Will you pour us a drink? I want to show you something." She nods and kicks off her heels, padding across the carpet barefoot, heading for the sideboard that holds a bottle of single malt and several tumblers. I turn and walk down the hall to the bedroom, opening my closet.

Returning to the living room, she's curled up on the couch, staring out the windows at the night sky. Our drinks are on the coffee table in front of her, but I ignore them and sit down. Pulling her legs onto my lap, I enjoy the trail of goosebumps that pop up as I lightly stroke my fingers up her thigh to the hem of her skirt and back down to her knee. She sighs happily, reaching out a hand to stroke the edge of my jaw with her fingers, I turn my head and lay a kiss in her palm.

"My tattoo says Nox inveniat. It means 'find the night.'" Her eyes meet mine and gleam in the darkness. She doesn't speak, waiting for me to continue.

"My father told me to find my night. He called my mother

112

his night every day of their marriage," my voice has gone low with emotion and I stare at my hand, still stroking her thigh.

"He said I would know I'd found love when I found the woman I wanted to spend not only my days, but every last one of my nights with," I pause and look into her eyes, trusting her with my heart. "And I found you Bree."

I offer her a small velvet box. She gasps, a hand fluttering up to her mouth, the other one shaking as she takes the box.

"Will you marry me?"

"Yes," she squeaks, "Yes, I love you, yes!"

Throwing her arms around my neck, she crawls in my lap and she's kissing me, and we're murmuring promises, and at some point she's also crying, her beautiful eyes brimming over, tears clinging to her lashes.

Eventually, realizing she's still holding the box in her hand, she leans back a tiny bit and opens it carefully. A two-carat black diamond on a delicate gold band winks at her from the velvet cushion.

"Ohhhhh," she breathes, her eyes flying up to mine and then back to the ring. "It's beautiful." I smile, loving her reaction and take the box from her hand. Removing the ring, I slide it on her finger. It's a perfect fit. I lay a kiss on her knuckles and look into her eyes.

"I'll love you forever," I whisper. She leans in close, her breath tickling my ear.

"Forever and ever." she whispers back.

What's in a Name?

Bree

Waking up in Nick's arms, I immediately pull my hand out from under the covers to make sure it wasn't all a dream. The black diamond twinkles at me reassuringly. It is so utterly perfect, I can't stop looking at it. It's emerald cut and *enormous,* with a thin gold band and filigree work all through the basket where the diamond sits.

Nick stirs behind me, running a hand up my back and around my ribs to cup my breast. He kisses the back of my neck and I feel him hard against my hip. Rolling over to face him, I slide my leg over his hip, pushing him onto his back as I straddle him. His eyes burn into mine as his hands grip my hips and I begin to rock, slow at first then faster as I feel heat building deep in my belly.

His hands squeeze my hips, pumping me even faster as a groan escapes his lips and I rock harder, grinding on his body. I feel the spiral take me and I climax hard, throwing my head back, feeling my nipples tighten as Nick comes with a roar underneath me. My vision fades to sparkles as I rock, riding the wave until I collapse forward onto his chest and his arms wrap around me as I remember how to breathe.

"Good morning, future-wife." His voice rumbles my ear through his chest, and I smile, sitting up enough to kiss him.

"Oh I love the sound of that," I giggle, "want me to put Margo on speaker phone later when I call to tell her the news?" He laughs and nods, "At least now she can stop hinting at how beautiful spring colors look on her skin tone." I roll my eyes dramatically.

"I'm excited to tell my parents," I chatter, rolling off him and curling up to his side, his fingers idly start a soft slow pattern on my arm, the light touch sending tingles straight to my brain. He clears his throat lightly and I glance up to see what might be a guilty smile.

"That surprise I might have spoiled, Love," he smiles and continues to stroke my arm, "I asked your father's permission the other night." *Ohmygod he is so perfect. SO PERFECT. And brave. I love this man.*

"I love you," I sigh, giving his chest a squeeze, smiling as I think about my plans. Three more days. *Two can play this game of surprising each other with awesomeness.*

The phone call to Margo is hilarious, and I do put Nick on speaker phone to enjoy the combination of shrieks and cursing as she begins planning our wedding.

"Okay Sugarpop, I'm gonna let you go, I've got so much to do! I'll call you when I have options for your dress narrowed down, oh my god, and cake! Kisses! Bye!" Margo disconnects without waiting for me to respond, and we burst out laughing.

"So, *Sugarpop*, I hope Margo has good taste, because it sounds like she just put herself in charge of your wedding," Nick laughs, and I poke him in the ribs.

"She'll calm down, and just you wait, she nicknames *everybody*," I wiggle my eyebrows dramatically, laughing at his look of consternation.

"You're lucky though, she already nicknamed you 'Mr. Perfect' a while ago-," I stop, glancing at him.

"Did she? How long ago?" His grin turns mischievous and his eyes narrow. *Well crap, oh whatever.*

"Well, let's just say Margo has been with us since day one." I blush harder, laughing. "You made quite an impression in your kitchen, all those muscles and ink and sweat and just a pair of shor-" his lips steal the rest of my words as he kisses me hard, hands knotting in my hair. *He is a fantastic fucking kisser. Seriously. Wow.*

Kissing leads to our clothes falling off again, and he kisses every bit of me...*that's code for he banged my brains out, it was amazing.*

The Surprise

Nick

*A*s we drive up the tree-lined drive, I assume Bree is quiet because we're heading out to Mrs. Henderson's house to pick up the last of her things. She's staring out the window, lost in her own thoughts. We park and walk up towards the house and she turns to me.

"So I have some news," she pauses, biting her lip, "this is all, well…mine." Sweeping an arm around at the house and the grounds, she looks at me, smiling. "Mrs. Henderson left it all to me, plus enough money to fix it the way it should be and a lot more. A LOT, a lot. Um, I've got some plans…that's what I've been doing for the past couple days, trying to get things started. I wanted to surprise you." She touches a finger to my lips, "don't say anything yet, I want to show you."

Taking my hand, she leads me past the main house, back to the carriage house. Sliding open the huge double doors she leads me in and we walk up to a large work table centered in the middle, several large papers held down by a tape measure fluttering in the breeze. A beam of sunlight cuts through the gloom, hitting the table. Sifting through the papers, Bree picks one to lay on top of the pile, setting the tape measure back on the corner to hold them down.

"So this is the original carriage house here, and this is the part I've been working on with a guy who specializes in historical renovations to modify." She points, and I lean closer. According to the drawings, the double doors leading out the back of the carriage house will now lead into an attached structure that is two levels surrounding an atrium. *She's building me a fucking gallery.* She keeps talking because she doesn't realize my heart is about to fucking burst.

"Are you building a gallery for me, Bree?" I grit out, my throat tight.

"Well, I hope you'll let me," her words tumble over each other, "the rest of my plan is that the front of the house is really formal and Randall didn't want any of the furniture, he just took some of the smaller things, so it's still all perfect, and the kitchen's commercial, so I thought maybe we could work together and have really special gallery shows…that start with really good dinners," she tapers off, "It was just an idea…maybe you'd rather have something different," she finishes quietly, staring at me.

She's building us a life, I don't know what I did to deserve this but I'm taking it and never letting go.

"I will spend the rest of my days trying to make you as happy as you make me," I can't say anymore, my throat is tight, my heart is so full. Her smile lights up the gloom as she dives into my arms. I sweep her right off her feet, her arms lock around my neck as I kiss her, and I never want to stop.

Final Romp at the Loft

Nick

T he last of my things are unloaded, and Bree and I look at each other and I reach for her hand. We've taken our time over the last couple of weeks deciding what to keep, designing the gallery space, rearranging some of the living spaces in the main house.

Mrs. Henderson's room has been converted back to an office for Bree. We've taken the largest bedroom on the second floor for ourselves. Mrs. Henderson's blue velvet recliner now lives in the attic, Bree put it near one of the windows overlooking the construction of the gallery.

The wedding plans are well underway, Margo is in her element, and contrary to Bree's prediction, Margo has not, in fact, calmed down one iota. She's got tremendous taste though, and I pulled her aside and let her know that she needs to ignore any budgets Bree set. Bree still hasn't wrapped her head around how much money we have between us. We're going to do this once, and we're going to do this right.

We walk out of the house to my jeep and drive into the city for one more walk-through of the loft. Walking through the empty rooms, I'm not going to miss anything except maybe the kitchen. *The place I first saw Bree and my world changed, the place I found my night.*

Bree walks into the kitchen and leans on the counter, crooking a finger at me with a sexy smile. I close the gap, finding the button of her jeans, I pop it open and slide them off, her panties follow. She kicks them off her feet as she's undoing the button of my jeans. I grab her ass and squeeze before sliding my hands under her thighs and lifting her up. She hisses and then moans as her skin hits the cold steel counter, her knees open wide.

And Babies Make Four

Bree

It's raining as we leave the loft, and we ride in easy silence. Nick's strong hand is on my thigh, and I'm lightly stroking his arm, tracing the ridges of his muscles with my fingers. It would not be possible for me to be happier right now. I look up at his profile as he drives, and his strong jaw twitches as he glances at me, the corner of his mouth quirking up.

We're on the outskirts of the city, nearing the house, when suddenly his eyes narrow, and his head swings around looking back at the road behind us as he slows the jeep down.

"Nick, what-" I'm startled, looking around to see what's happening. He pulls the jeep over and puts it in park, unbuckling his seatbelt.

"Just sit tight a second, I thought I saw something," he mutters jumping out of the jeep and running back down the road through the rain. He stops and kneels near a rain culvert plunging his arm in, bringing out something small. Reaching in again, he pulls out what looks like a handful of mud. Running back to the jeep, he stops at the back and opens it, grabbing a blanket.

"Nick, what-!" He carefully hands me the blanket and the bedraggled kittens inside meow plaintively.

"Oh my god, how did you see them in the rain? Oh, you're all soaked," I cuddle the kittens up, rubbing them carefully with one end of the blanket as Nick laughs and uses the other end to mop off his face before getting the jeep back on the road.

"I saw them fall off the edge of the culvert right as we drove by." The kittens are calming down, purring so loud their tails are vibrating as they stand and start to investigate. Both females, one is gray with white paws and a little blaze of white right between her blue eyes. Her little claws hook into my shirt as she crawls right up to my neck, turns around and lays under my hair on my shoulder, purring in my ear. The other is pure black with golden eyes, she kneads her little claws on my thigh, tiny little pinpricks, before curling up in my lap and closing her eyes.

"I think they've adopted you," Nick smiles, glancing at us as he pulls up the driveway. "They look old enough to be away from their mama, if you want to keep them."

"They're perfect," I nod, touching Black's sweet little nose. Wrapping them in the blanket again, we run to the house. Drying the kittens off, we let them explore while we shower and change into dry clothes.

As I leave the bedroom to head back downstairs, I hear a

squeaky little 'mrowl?' disappearing upstairs to the attic. Nick walks out behind me in jeans, no shirt, toweling off his hair. *Yum.* Dropping the towel around his neck, he follows me up the stairs and we look for the kittens, who, of course, have now fallen silent.

At the end of the attic, under the big half moon window, I find them, curled up in Mrs. H's blue velvet recliner, purring. Nick walks up behind me, sliding his arms around my waist and kissing the top of my head. We stand together, looking out the window at the beginnings of the gallery, his heat at my back, and nothing could be more perfect. *Speaking of...*I dissolve into giggles looking down at the kittens.

"What's so funny?" Nick's chest vibrates against my back and I turn in his arms, grabbing both ends of the towel to pull his face down to mine for a kiss.

"Nothing, I was just remembering something." *Hope my clothes don't randomly fall off...well, that would actually be very okay.* "They're just fucking adorable."

"*You're* fucking adorable," he laughs, kissing the tip of my nose.

"I fucking love you, Nick," I giggle, tilting my face up for another kiss.

"I fucking love you too, Sugarpop," he grins, kissing me as I smile into his lips.

II

Part 2: A Night Wedding

Margo's On the Job

Three Months After the Proposal

Bree

"*I* know you're excited Margo, but please, please, *please* can you rein it in? For me?" I may as well be talking to a wall, Margo's attention is focused on the tablet in her lap. She's got a notebook full of scribbling, a pen stuck behind each ear, and four empty espresso cups scattered around like an abandoned tea party. Picking up one of her discarded little balls of paper, I toss it at her, bouncing it off the top of her head.

"Hmm what? Oh, rein it in, yeah, got it chiclet," she starts to focus on the tablet again but gives her head a little shake and suddenly her eyes are on me like lasers. "Wait, why would you need to tell me to rein it in? This isn't even wedding stuff." She flips the tablet face down in her lap before I can see, looking guilty.

Giving up with a sigh, I grab my purse off the chair I tossed it in when I arrived. I dig out my keys and look at Margo again.

"And what I meant was, rein it in tonight when you meet Williams?" I hate asking, but sometimes she is just so...*Margo.* "He can be kind of uptight, and you're going to have to work together a little, he's Nick's best man." Margo rewards me with an eye roll.

"I'm not going to shock and awe the silver fox tonight," she huffs, "so unclench." She scribbles a quick note before tucking the pen back behind her ear. I'm clearly dismissed.

"Silver fox?" I can't stifle the nervous giggle that bubbles out. "Oh geez... so you'll meet us downtown? Emilio's at eight?" Margo flashes a smile at me and waves me out the door.

"I'll be there Sugarpop, and stop worrying, best behavior." She crosses her heart with a finger, kisses the tip and blows it at me. Laughing, I give up and catch it before heading out the door.

The projects at the mansion are almost complete, just tiny details left, and Nick and I are anxious to have our first gallery night. But first, our wedding. The first event in the carriage house that has been expanded into a gallery space will be our wedding, and that is the only detail besides the flavor of the cake that Margo has allowed me.

"Well you being a foodie, probably you get to okay the cake," she snarked at me when she hauled me into the tasting, "but that's it, the rest you leave to me."

As if I have a choice. Margo and Nick conspired together and decided to do things out of order. Tonight we have dinner with Margo and Williams so that they can meet and begin working together to finalize the wedding arrangements. Their meeting is long overdue, but Williams has been travelling with his daughter Laurel, joking about early retirement.

Tomorrow morning I step on a plane, destination tropical, with Nick. My honeymoon is happening before the wedding. One month of relaxation and lots and lots of time spent naked. We come back a week before the wedding when, according to Margo, 'all will be revealed' *cue mysterious eyebrow wriggle.*

"Just make sure you come back well-rested." Margo clucked at me, "and no weird tan lines."

Nick was a little less sure I would go along with this scheme. Tonight, after dinner, as we curl up in a big lounge chair on the balcony under the stars, he links our fingers together and kisses my knuckles.

"Love, if you want to be here to do wedding stuff, say the word," he murmurs, kissing my hand again. Turning on my side to face him I smile and shake my head.

"No, honestly, this is genius. You and me, alone, travelling, and we come back for our wedding? I can't think of anything better than leaving all this to Margo and getting far, far away." We laugh together as his arms slide around me and he pulls me into a hug on top of him.

The best part about living outside of the city? I sit up, straddling him, and he shoves the hem of the nightie I'm wearing up on my hips. I gasp as I feel a pull and then hear the snap, and my underwear become a ripped scrap of lace on the floor beside us. I raise up on my knees and he smiles at me as he shoves his shorts off his hips.

I feel him, hard and ready, underneath me. Grabbing the hem of my nightie, I toss it off over my head. The night air tickles my skin and my nipples harden. We move together, slow at first and then harder, faster. The night is quiet, and the only sounds I hear are our quickening breaths and the slide of skin on skin.

Nick's fingers dig into my hips and he moves even faster, his eyes intense until I feel the wave building and I let my head drop back, pumping my hips as my vision blurs. Grounded by the feel of his chest under my hands, his heart pounding with mine, the wave crashes over me.

I keep moving as I feel him shudder and jerk up into me hard, his eyes slide closed and his hands squeeze my hips again before sliding loose onto my thighs. Eyes still shut, he smiles, hands sliding back up my legs to my ribs as he pulls me down onto his chest. Tilting my face up to his, he kisses me slow and long.

"So…a month of this?" Nick groans, squeezing me tight, "I might never bring you back."

"It would probably be best if you did," I can't help but laugh as I picture the fallout. "If the temptation is too great, just imagine the wrath of Margo if you foil her plans for our wedding." He laughs along with me, and my world is perfect.

Taming the Silver Fox

Margo

I am going to kill him. I swear on my mother, if that man sticks his nose in my wedding planning beeswax *one more time*. Death by fonging. *I heard that on a movie once.* I will fong that man dead.

"Okay douche-pickle, let's try this again," I blow out a sigh, "obviously my ability to be diplomatic has taken a hiatus, and my patience isn't far behind." His dark eyebrows draw together as he stares at me in annoyed disbelief.

"I'm going to need you to hand me that credit card before you do any more damage today, Margo," he's speaking slowly and clearly as if I'm a kindergartener instead of a grown woman.

"There's not a chance in tea-length-chiffon-hell of me giving you this card," I'm literally hissing the words and I'm so tempted to stomp my foot it's almost physically painful. He is infuriating. Utterly infuriating. Three months of wedding planning and now, every detail, every fabric, every color, every scent, every flavor... Scrutinized, questioned, *in some instances mocked* during the last week. Every. Damn. Thing.

"Then it seems we are at an impasse," his deep voice is stern and he folds his arms. I ignore the little bloom of heat bursting in my chest because, *of course*, he's in a suit. While the coat is slung over the back of a chair, folding his arms like that does delightful things to his biceps and the irritated bunching of his shoulder muscles. *For fuckssake Margo, focus, stupid suit fetish, oh my god he's even wearing cufflinks; and now my uterus just decided to do a backflip, god, focus.*

"I'm pretty sure *impasse* means a point where neither of us will be getting our way and that's where you are mistaken, *Sanford*," I hammer the formality of his name simply because I know he hates it. I'm rewarded with a small grimace and tightening of his jaw.

"For about the eight-hundredth time," I roll my eyes and reach out, *mostly because I can't stop myself at this point,* and poke him in the chest with one ruby-red fingernail. "This is Bree's wedding," *poke,* "and given the lack of faith in the sanctity of marriage," *poke,* "demonstrated by society in recent years," *poke,* "in truly the most romantic moment I have ever witnessed, your best friend, who is THE GROOM, made one of the sweetest indirect declarations of love I have ever heard," *poke.* "He said, *and I quote*, 'I'm only doing this once, we're going to do it right,' end quote," *poke,* "directly tied to a discussion about the budget of this wedding." *Poke.*

I stop talking, not because I want to, rather because I'm horribly out of breath at this point in my tirade. Catching sight of his face, the little smirk on his lips gives me my second wind. *How dare he smirk when I'm on a roll?!*

Absently rubbing his chest, Sanford Williams is staring somewhere over my shoulder as he shakes his head in amusement. With my silence, his eyes flick down to meet mine and he sees my mouth fly open to launch into round two. Quickly he reaches out and lays his hand across my mouth. Lifting his other hand to his own mouth, one finger pointed, he gives me the universal symbol for 'shush'.

"I was simply trying to lead you towards the way of thinking that a fourth truckload of flowers might be overkill," he clips off each word, not taking his hand off my mouth. "Once again, your sanctity of marriage and declaration of love speech wins the day. I yield." He stares at me hard for a moment, and *because I'm a childish asshole,* I lick his palm.

Yanking his hand away with a funny little yelp, he stares at me for a long moment and then abruptly turns on his heel and storms out of the room. *That was easy,* turning back to my tablet and endless scribblings, I continue checking off last minute details with a smile.

A Bumpy Beginning

One Week Later

Williams

When Nick railroaded me into providing assistance, *as what can only realistically be called Margo's flunkey,* I had no idea what I was getting myself into. I had no idea weddings were such productions, and yet Margo assures me that this wedding will be nothing but classic and simple.

The woman has been in my office every day for one week straight. I don't know what she does for a living, but apparently it affords her plenty of time to torment me. She came to my house on the weekend, I still don't know how she found the address. The details, the calls, the money spent, more details. I swear, if I ever decide to start another business, I'm hiring her and then leaving the country. *Nick and Bree were onto something.*

My own wedding was a drunken affair in Vegas, I was young and stupid. Tanya was beautiful and happy and had eyes only for me. We had Laurel and ten good years. The divorce was messy. Tanya is married to a Greek shipping magnate now, and by all accounts doing well. Laurel looks like her mother, and that used to make my heart ache. It's been years and now I'm just glad she's happy.

When Nick and Bree got engaged and finding a new gallery space became a non-issue, I was without an immediate purpose for the first time in my life. For so many years after the divorce, I devoted myself to being a good father and filled the rest of my hours with work. After the initial engagement whirlwind, Nick and I met for drinks and a cigar as we'd done so many nights when his father was alive.

"Bree and I want you to be a part of our new venture," Nick's eyes were earnest, his voice sincere. He sipped his whiskey and waited for my response.

"Not this one, Nick. This project is for you and Bree, and I can't even tell you how happy I am that you've found her," I stopped to take a drink, choosing my next words. "I think it's time for me to do some travelling, call it a bit of an early retirement," we both laughed, knowing I'll never be able to truly stop working. "I'm going to take a break, figure out my next move." He nodded and we sat in silence, sipping our whiskey and watching the smoke curl up into the air.

I took Laurel to all the places she mentioned as a child that we hadn't seen yet, and did several solo trips when she was occupied elsewhere. I came back refreshed and ready to take on the world again. Little did I know I would have my hands full of the whirlwind that is Margo.

The woman could legitimately be classified as a natural disaster. She's bossy and domineering and relentless. If I didn't know any better I would think she was planning the invasion of a mid-size country rather than a wedding. She's also unpredictable. *The hand lick was unexpected.* I've come to look forward to our verbal sparring matches, she never fails to disappoint.

As if she can hear me thinking about her, my phone beeps. The woman always texts. It's tedious, but, because it's Margo, never boring.

Margo: I think it's time we start over.

Start over...good grief. Why would she want to start over? Things are fine as they are, we bicker over wedding details and money. End of story.

Me: Why?
  (delete)
  Me: I don't think that's necessary.
  (delete)
  Me: Stop being ridiculous, starting over implies a relationship that does not exist in these circumstances, after the wedding you can forget I exist.
  (DELETE)

I set the phone aside without replying, frustrated. Heaving out a sigh I grab the phone again.

Me: What did you have in mind?

Tossing the phone aside again, I head for the pool. I'm going to swim laps until I'm mentally prepared for whatever that crazy woman wants next.

Let's Try This Again

Margo

I stare at my phone, annoyed. I told Williams we need a reset and he didn't tell me to get bent, which was actually kind of a shock, and then nothing. I stare at the screen, willing him to respond.

> Me: I think it's time we start over.
> SW: What did you have in mind?
> Me: Are you busy right now?

Nothing. It's like he's the master of finding the best way to make me go nuts. I leave my phone on the counter and walk away, trying not to be so damn anxious. I simply feel that *perhaps* I was too antagonizing with Williams when we met, and things have been tense ever since.

It's not that I don't enjoy our spats, he doesn't give an inch. The man is clever and well-spoken, and the mocking comments and snide remarks roll out of his mouth in the sexiest cultured rumble. It doesn't matter what he says, his voice makes everything sound hot, and then all my girl bits tense up hoping to get some action and it's hard to think straight.

Not that I'm attracted to him. I'm not. I'm NOT. *That's a lie. Every estrogen-soaked fiber of my being thinks he is sexy as all hell and wants me to play nice, like, yesterday.*

Ever since he walked up to the table at Emilio's and shook my hand, I've been a smitten-kitten. It's ridiculous, it's not like it's been *that* long since my last date. I mean, I wouldn't want to do the math or anything, but...*yeah...it's been a while.*

"And how does Margo react when having involuntary feelings?" I ask myself in the hall mirror. "Well, since you asked, Margo, she turns into a crazy, detail obsessed hellcat with zero sense of personal space and zero regard for the feelings of the person who attracted her. Because that makes sense. Drive them away quickly." I roll my eyes at myself in the mirror.

My phone pings. *Finally.*

SW: I apologize for the delay, I was swimming. No, I'm not busy.

Swimming huh? Well that explains why he fills out a suit so nicely. *I should have sex with him. SHUT UP HORMONES, NO ONE INVITED YOU TO THIS PARTY. But yeah, sex with him would probably be pretty great.* Sigh.

Me: Finley's on 4th? In an hour?

It's weird how nervous I am…I feel like I just asked him on a date. I wonder what he's thinking right now.

Ping.

SW: Agreed.

Eye roll.

The Do-Over

Williams

I haven't set foot in Finley's in years, but the old wood bar still shines and the noise of the batting cages in the back is music to my ears. Glancing around, I don't see Margo, but I'm a little early. Heading for the bar, I see they have an English brown ale on tap that I haven't tried, I order a pint and find a seat where I'll see Margo when she arrives.

This business of starting over has me puzzled. I'm curious to see what she has in mind. I honestly don't see the point as we won't be crossing paths often, if ever, when the wedding is over. However, it would be arrogant to blow off the opportunity not to bicker with her on a daily basis. A more cordial working relationship, if that is indeed Margo's goal, would be preferable to our current situation.

Musing over my beer, I almost miss her entrance. Margo doesn't see me right away. It feels like an opportunity to appreciate her without listening to the barrage of outraged squawking that would ensue if she caught me staring. She looks for meaning in every word, every look, every gesture. Everything has to be explained. It's rather exhausting, and so I take a moment to enjoy looking at the woman approaching the bar.

It amuses me that Margo is related to Bree. Bree has long, wavy-blonde hair and pale skin, she's average height, too slender for my taste. She's happy and bubbly and clever and cute. I can see why Nick is taken with her, they are the perfect balance. She is everything he needs when he gets too serious, too quiet, works too hard.

Margo has a short cap of loose dark curls, huge brown eyes, and full lips. She's short, I would guess barely over five feet tall, built like a pin-up girl with a derriere a sculptor would shed a happy tear over. Tonight she's wearing tight jeans, little red sneakers instead of her usual heels, and a low-cut red t-shirt.

She leans up on the bar so that the bartender can hear her order, and after he hands her a beer she turns to survey the crowd. Her mouth forms a little 'O' of surprise, gone as quickly as it appeared, when she sees me. Her smile seems nervous as she crosses the room.

I stand up to meet her as she approaches the table, and her step falters just a tiny bit as a blush creeps up her neck to stain her cheeks. Tossing her head, she recovers quickly and gives me a cheeky grin.

"I should have figured you'd be early," tossing back a gulp of beer she looks me over. Ignoring the little dig, I take a drink of my beer and wait, it doesn't take long.

"Well, whatever. You look nice. It's kind of weird to see you without your suit." Her tone is softer, friendlier. I give her a small smile and take another drink of beer. *She'll get to the point of this...eventually...I hope.* She huffs out a sigh, and I hide another smile, the only battles I ever win with Margo are the ones I refuse to participate in by remaining silent.

"So...you're probably wondering why I wanted to meet you..." she glances at me for confirmation before continuing, I give her eye contact. "Well, as much as I enjoy this argue first, last and again later relationship we've established..." she grins to soften her words, "I was thinking that maybe I've been pushing your buttons a little hard." Her tone is light, and I keep my eyes on her face, willing her to continue.

"Anyway, I just thought...maybe we could hang out?" This uncertain, soft-spoken Margo is confusing me, *hang out?* I realize she's now silent, waiting for me to take a turn speaking. Glancing out the window at the passersby, I'm uncertain what to say, and afraid that I'm woefully unpracticed at 'hanging out'.

"I would agree that our relationship has been...a little more adversarial than I had anticipated when tasked with providing my assistance." I pause to take another swallow of beer and, glancing at her, find her gaze fixed firmly on my mouth. *Curious.*

"I'm afraid my college years are far behind me, and I am well out of practice in 'hanging out', but I would welcome the opportunity to explore this new-found...camaraderie?" *She is still staring at my mouth. Now she's smiling, I don't know what that means, I'm terrible at this.*

"You're such a dork...I could listen to you talk forever," her eyes are focused on my lips and her expression is decidedly dreamy as she almost sighs the words. *I'm a dork? How so? But she likes...what...my voice? Could she possibly be...no...well... maybe...is she flirting?* When I don't respond she snaps back to attention.

"Wow...I didn't mean to say that out loud." Taking a nervous gulp of her beer, she looks around the bar. "I hope this place is okay, my friends and I used to go to the college baseball games and this is where the team hung out after, it was a lot of fun."

"Yes, it's fine." I'm almost afraid to talk, because that dreamy-faced Margo made me exceedingly nervous.

"Yeah...I made things weird...so...want to go hit a few in the cages?" She nods at the batting cages visible through the back windows and fixes me with a devilish look.

"That must be a yes," she mutters, when I stand, grab my beer and head for the back. I'll do pretty much anything at this point to avoid sitting here suffering through this awkward conversation. Stopping at the bar, I order a pitcher of beer to be sent to us in the back. I turn to see Margo glance back at me with a little smile as she pushes through the door.

Let the Games Begin

Margo

"*L*adies first." Setting his beer on the table, Williams leans against the wall and waves me through the gate, He crosses his arms over his chest and gives me the smallest smile, just a twitch of his lips. He looks more at ease now than he did sitting at the table, and it's hard to reconcile this untucked Williams with the stern guy in the suit I've been dealing with all week.

He's wearing dark jeans that strain just a tiny bit around muscular thighs and a short sleeve button-down in a white and light green plaid that sets off his tan *really nicely*. His thick, dark hair has mostly gone silver and he's got strong sharp features. *And right now he's watching me and starting to get that skittish look on his face again so it's time to stop admiring and get with the program.*

"It's been a while since I've done this," I admit, "I might not be any good anymore." Selecting a bat, I step up and get into position, pushing the button. *I wonder if he's checking out my ass...I hope so, almost as much as I hope I can hit this ball.*

Swinging at the first ball, I smile at the 'crack' as the bat makes contact. *Still got it.* We've got it set on the warm up, so I don't have to aim at anything, but I start trying to pick my spots as I hit. These cages feature a game with a large target at the end of the cage. After he does a few warm up hits I'm going to challenge him, *because challenging people is in my DNA,* and because I want to show off a little.

I hit a few more before I stop the machine and step back, glancing over my shoulder. His gaze is appreciative, and a little surprised, as he pushes off of the wall. A pitcher of beer is on the table and he pours me one before heading over to get a bat. He takes a minute to look at them, choosing one and taking a few practice swings. He's not paying attention to me at this point, so I'm free to stare and *oh yeahhhh, that's hot.*

Stepping up, he pushes the button and starts to hit...and never misses. He's good. Like, really good. After six or seven he steps back, turning to look at me and I snap my mouth shut before I drool, trying to smile nonchalantly.

"Looks like you've played before," I want to sound sexy but I feel like I sound kind of squeaky. *And what kind of lame-ass line was that, god.* He smiles, a real, honest smile, and shrugs in a super-cute way that makes my hoo-ha tingle as he walks over to me. Reaching for his beer on the table just behind me, he leans close enough that I can smell his cologne. *Down girl, don't jump him, he just for-real smiled at you, don't screw it up.*

"It's been a long time, but I used to play...quite a bit actually."

His eyes crinkle as he smiles again, "Did you want to play the target game?" With a look that is decidedly challenging, he's turned the tables on me, *and I like it.*

"Oh, you're on, let's see what you've got," I counter and walk over to set the machine.

A Detour Down Memory Lane

Williams

*M*argo takes the first turn, five swings, scoring on all of them, including one homerun. Watching her, the concentration on her face and the line of her shoulders and hips as she swings, she's beautiful. I find myself wishing she was awful so I could step up behind her in one of those terrible movie scenarios, helping her hold the bat, giving me a reason to touch her. *Where did that come from?*

While I've always been aware of Margo, *it would be impossible not to be,* I've never acknowledged that I might be attracted to her. I don't tend to think about many women that way, I've been single for a long time. The occasional date, business lunch that turns friendly, short relationships, nothing serious because I never allow it to get that far. I'm too easily disappointed.

As she turns to me, eyes bright, I can't help but smile back. She exaggerates the swing of her hips as she saunters over to the table, cocky, and hands me the bat.

"Show me what you go-" her voice is drowned out by a loud male voice behind me.

"Well holy-shit, I told you boys! That's Ford Williams! Ford! Man, it's been a *long* time!" Voice booming across the cages, the man has a red face, thinning blonde hair, and a barrel chest. He holds both arms out as he walks towards me, followed by three other men. Staring at him for a moment, I finally put a name to his face and allow him to pull me into a one-armed hug.

"Scott Butler, how are you?" I'm internally groaning, this isn't a reunion I would choose to have with Margo present.

"Livin' the dream son! Beer, broads and baseball, you know the drill! You boys go get some beer." He waves his friends off to the bar as he lets go of me and spies Margo. His eyes rove over her in a way I don't like at all, and he gives her a leer, "Yep, you know the drill, good man." As Margo's mouth opens with what is sure to be an epic retort, I step to her side and slide an arm around her waist.

"I'm long past those days Scott, this is Margo and you owe her an apology." Glancing down at her, I watch her lips close softly and the tiniest hint of pink appears high on her cheeks.

"Well shit, my apologies Margo, you know me Ford, always opening my trap without thinking, no harm intended." Scott claps me on the shoulder and waves at the waitress to bring him a beer. Margo's back is stiff, but I feel her relax a tiny bit and her hand slides around my waist, the side of her body tucked into mine.

"Beer, broads and baseball, huh?" The tone of Margo's voice is dangerous, not at all in keeping with the warmth of her at my side or the light play of her fingers on my back.

"Oh, just our little joke," Scott blusters, "me and Ford go way back, see, but I haven't seen him for, what's it been Ford? 25 years?" He drains his glass, pouring another off the pitcher and resting his elbows on the table with a sigh.

"At least that, I haven't kept track," It's difficult to keep my tone friendly. I don't know how to extricate Margo and I from this impending trip down memory lane, and she's quiet beside me which is never a good thing with Margo.

"Oh, that's the way it is, I know," Scott nods sagely over his beer and then his eyes sharpen on the bat leaning on the wall.

"You still any good?" He nods at the bat and then scrutinizes me, "looks like you're staying in shape, can you still hit the ball like you used to?"

"When did you two play together?" Margo cuts in, curious.

"Oh we played in high school, all the way through college, and that there is when I was done, pretty lady," Scott muses. "Ford here, he was the real deal, got tapped for the big leagues," he sighs, "then he found himself in the family way with his little woman. Decided he couldn't handle all the travelling, and that was that." Scott toasts us and drains another glass.

"That was a long time ago," I don't know what else to say. It feels like another lifetime, and I don't like looking back. Those were the years Tanya and I were happy, the years that gave me Laurel, and then it was over. Margo seems to sense my mood is tanking, because she gives my waist a squeeze. Looking up at me consideringly, her hand slides to my butt and gives *it* a squeeze as well.

"Well?" Margo playfully swats my butt and slides away from

me, reaching for her beer. "Can you still hit the ball like you used to? How about you and Scott go head to head? Winner owes me a dance." Lifting her beer in a toast to us both, she hops up on one of the stools by the table outside the cage.

"I'll play," Scott sets his glass down hard and ambles over to the bats, choosing one, he points it at Margo, "that dance is mine, pretty lady." Walking over to the machine he resets it and starts the game.

Ohmygod I Did That

Margo

F ord. *Now that's a good nickname, why the hell didn't he ever tell me to call him that?* His face is stony as he looks at Scott's back and then walks over to me, leaning close as he grabs the bat I left leaning against the wall. Straightening, he turns his head to mine. I feel his breath on my ear, the tiniest shiver races up the backs of my arms.

"What's your game, Margo?" His velvet voice has an edge to it that I like. *Very much.*

"Maybe I'm just looking for a way to get a dance with you," I hate that I sound so breathy, but I'm so hot for him right now that there is real potential for spontaneous combustion and I really want him to touch me again. I see his jaw tense, and he swallows. *Maybe he's a little hot for me too...* and without thinking, I lean forward and nip his earlobe and then flutter a tiny kiss on the side of his neck.

We both freeze for a millisecond, *ohmygod I did that, ohmygod I just did that,* and then I turn away, reaching for my beer, giving him sexy side-eye…*is that a thing? I hope that's a thing, if it's not I look ridiculous right now. If he just walks away without a reaction of some kind, I will die. What if he's not into me?*

His tan can't hide the heat that creeps up his neck as he puts his hands on the table at my sides, caging me in, *that's hot.* He narrows his eyes, considering me.

"I'm not sure you can handle a dance with me Margo," his voice is low and rough and *ohmygod he went there. I need a fan… industrial-sized…pointed straight at my crotch right now.*

"Go win and we'll find out," I go for a sexy whisper this time, *it was a warble.* Grinning, he pushes off the table to play for a dance.

Play for a Dance

Williams

Scott is predictable and wants to show off. He picks a straight-forward game that tallies up points based on where you hit the target, the higher on the target the better, with the top several inches labelled 'home run 100'. *He thinks he's going to finish me off quickly with a high score... interesting.*

He's smart to choose this game. Back in our college days, Scott was known for being a heavy hitter. I was better at placing the ball in those sweet spots the outfielders couldn't get to in time. What Scott doesn't know was that I enjoyed the strategy and the technique rather than just swinging away... but that doesn't mean I won't do it to win.

"I was sorry to hear you and Tanya split," Scott tosses the

comment out callously, probably hoping to throw me off. We weren't that close in the past, more friendly competitors. I knew at the time that he would have taken Tanya's attention away from me if he could.

"Oh I doubt that," I lean on the bat and wave him forward for the first round. Scott smirks and swaggers up, pushing the button to start the machine. Each round is five hits, he's set it for two rounds.

I look over at Margo. She's watching me, and when I make eye contact, her full red lips silently mouth 'perfect' before parting in a smile. I stare at her for a second and then nod, trying to stop thinking about those lips on my skin. I don't know what she's playing at, *or if she's playing at all.*

The crack of Scott's bat as he hits the first ball jolts me back to the task at hand, the ball cleanly connects with the home run part of the target. He glances back to make sure Margo and I noticed.

"Scared yet Ford?" He turns back to the game without waiting for a response, just as the second ball launches, but his ego tripped him up because he rushes his swing. The ball thumps into the stripe below the home run. Scott's eyes narrow and he doesn't look at us. The last three balls thud, one after the other, right into the home run stripe.

"Gave you a little room to hope," Scott continues his cocky swagger, but his jaw is tight. He leans the bat on the cage wall and heads to the table while I step up for my turn.

"That was kind of you," I keep my tone light and glance at Margo, she gives me a wink. Smiling, I step up and start my turn. It's against my nature to be showy, but I'd say Scott has it coming at this point...and I want that dance. Five home run hits later, I step away and carefully lean my bat against the cage. Scott scowls, draining another glass of beer, wiping his mouth on the back of his hand as he stands.

"Ford always did want all the best things for himself," he muses, not looking at us as he steps up for his second turn, "…especially when it came to women." His face is serious as he starts the round. Five home run hits later, he turns with a smile.

"Guess it's my day." He tosses the bat near the rack and saunters back to the table, standing too close to Margo. I pause, wondering if I should tell him to back off, but…I should know better, it's *Margo's* personal space he's trying to invade.

"There's a whole *earth* here you know," her tone is friendly but firm, "go pick another piece to stand on, you haven't won yet." Laughing, Scott holds up both hands and retreats to the other side of the table. Smiling to myself I swing the bat. Five more home runs. Setting the bat aside I walk back to the table.

Margo's face is lit up with a 1000-watt smile and Scott looks like he ate something that didn't agree with him. I hear him mutter something that sounds like 'lucky bastard' as he pushes away from the table.

"It was good to see you again Scott, it's been too long." I hope he can hear that I mean it, even as I hope I don't run into him again for another 25 years.

"Sure thing Ford, enjoy your dance," his tone is sour as he stomps out of the cage with a nod at Margo. As soon as he's through the door we hear him hollering for beer as he bellies up to the bar with his buddies. Margo watches him go, and then turns to me.

"Keeping all the best things to yourself?" She's curious and I squelch an irritated sigh, annoyed that a chance run-in with Scott has led to a few more miles on memory lane.

"That's all old history, I'd say Scott never quite got over his crush on the woman we both liked...the woman I married." Keeping my tone light, I hope she'll drop the subject. No such luck.

"What's the story with you, divorced then?" Her tone is nothing but curious, and so I elaborate.

"Yes, divorced when my daughter Laurel was nine. Tanya has since remarried." I hope at this point that the story is boring enough for her to let it go. All the old hurt is gone, it's just memories at this point. Margo nods and sips her beer, thinking.

"Is there...anyone else? Are you dating anyone?" *Oh...this is worse, I'd rather talk about my divorce.*

"No." That's all she's getting, I don't know why she cares anyway, and I'm about to call it a night, dance or not.

"Sorry, sorry. We've never really talked before, you're not an easy person to get to know," she's nervous again, and I answer without thinking.

"What relevance could my dating history possibly have in the context of getting to know me?" I'm aware that my tone is hard, but I'm annoyed and can't stop the words. As I open my mouth to continue she cuts me off.

"Nothing, and I'm sorry I asked, geez, I didn't mean to get your panties in a bunch, I just want to get to know you. I realize now that I went at it from the wrong direction, obviously, but that was just a dumb way to figure out if you're single." Margo sucks in a breath and the words continue to tumble out as I stare at her, "I probably should have just said, 'hey, I think you're hot and awesome and we should go on a date', and then you could have made some scathing remark in your sexy man-voice, and then life could have just gone on, bu-" her next word is muffled as I gently lay my hand across her mouth.

My thoughts are racing, she stills under my touch and I feel her lips part as her tongue flicks out and touches my palm. Slowly I take my hand away, brushing my thumb across her full lower lip.

"That probably would have been the more straight-forward way to clue me in to your interest, yes." I respond slowly, trying to organize my thoughts. She rewards me with an exaggerated eye-roll.

"Yeah, a straight-forward way to get me sent off with a pat on the head. Duh. I'm not an idiot, Ford." Margo is sassy with nerves now that her feelings have been spilled out for me.

"Don't call me Ford," I mutter absently, still bemused at the turn this conversation has taken. She huffs out a sigh and I give her eye contact, snapping out of my reverie. "My apologies, that was rude, but I would prefer not to be referred to as Ford. It's a nickname that doesn't fit with my life anymore." Margo is subdued, an unusual look for her, but it doesn't last long.

"Well I'm not going to keep calling you Sanford, which you don't seem to like, which is why I was doing it, and it feels weird to call you Williams, like you're some kind of butler." She grabs her beer angrily, slopping some on the table before she takes a drink.

"Then you may call me whatever you like, it is unfortunate that I was not named in a manner to suit your tastes." Too cold, and I can't stop myself. I pull out my wallet and throw a few bills on the table. "Good night, Margo." Her eyes are huge and shining. I want to take it all back and let her call me Ford and pull her into my arms for that dance. Instead, I turn and leave the bar without looking back.

Oil and Water

Margo

Standing there, stunned, I watch his back as he exits the bar. How did this night end up going so completely wrong? Sitting back in the chair, I nurse my beer for a few minutes, thinking back over our conversation. Maybe we're just oil and water.

I've got a lot of nervous energy looking for an outlet at this point, so I grab a bat and start the pitching machine again. Ball after ball, thinking about nothing but swing and hit, I finally relax. When I step back, I can tell I'm pitting out and my hair feels damp with sweat. I turn to gather my stuff and leave, and Scott is there.

"In my experience, leaving your date behind at the end of the night means something went south," he drawls, but there's no burn to his words as he leans against the wall, slowly drinking his beer.

"You could say that," I shrug, no fight left in me at this point. "He doesn't want me to call him 'Ford' and that was the tipping point. I don't even know what happened." Huffing out a sigh I shoulder my purse. Scott barks out a laugh.

"I bet he doesn't, he's not really that guy anymore. I kept calling him Ford because I wanted to piss him off, but when him an' Tanya split he started going by Williams."

"What kind of guy was Ford?" I hang my purse back on the corner of my chair and sit down. Scott pulls out the other chair and sits across from me.

"Well, Ford was a young, stupid pup, just like the rest of us. Cocky because he was a baseball player. Went through the girls, not caring about much, it was different then." Scott's eyes are far away, remembering.

"Then one night, in this very bar, Tanya and her friends came in," he smiles, "she was pretty as a spring morning and he was a man on a mission. Flowers, poems, candies, you name it he did it, and pretty soon they were joined at the hip." Scott pauses, thinking.

"So what happened?" I wave my hand, impatient. *Ohmygod I brought him to the bar where he met his ex-wife.*

"They got married in Vegas and she turned up with a bun in the oven," Scott laughs. "Seemed like they were happy. By the time they split up I hadn't talked to him in a while. I heard the divorce was pretty bad, though." He pauses again, remembering. "Tanya walked away from Ford and left Laurel behind, she wanted to be a baseball player's wife, she wasn't ready to be a mom with a mortgage." Scott's face is somber at this point. "That was the end of Ford though, *Williams* was a serious guy, a father who didn't have time for any of our old shenanigans." He polishes off his beer and sets it on the table with a clink.

"Anyway, I don't know what happened between you two, but once upon a time we were friends, and I *can* tell you this," he points one finger at me, a tiny sway giving away how much he's had to drink. *Probably enough to make him completely honest.* "There's not a better man out there, and he raised up that girl by himself, and he deserves a good woman." Turning his head to release a belch, Scott sketches a wave in my direction and saunters back to the bar.

So…*unintentionally* I did just about everything possible to make this the most awkward evening ever. Great.

Night Swimming

Williams

I t's been three days since I left Margo at the bar. She hasn't contacted me once. No calls, no texts, no bursting into my office with a list of demands. Nothing. *I shouldn't have walked out, it's just a stupid nickname, I should have told her why it mattered.* I sent a text last night, a simple, 'I'm sorry'…no response.

Staring moodily at the pool, I listen to the waterfall at the end splash and bubble. Swirling the ice in my glass, I wonder if I'll be able to sleep. Standing abruptly, I head inside, leaving the door open to the cool night air. Setting my glass on the counter with a clink, I wander through the house, turning off lights, locking the front door.

As I pass through the kitchen in the dark, I'm surprised when the outdoor lights around the pool come on. At first I assume a deer must have wandered in, the lights are set not to notice small animals, then I hear a startled 'Eep!' and a splash.

Pulling the door open wider, I quickly walk out to the pool, scanning the area. A small pile of clothes near the far corner of the pool catches my attention, and I see a phone sitting near the edge of the pool. As I walk closer, Margo comes up for air, staying in the water to her chin near the wall of the pool.

"Um, hi," her voice is small, embarrassed.

"Good evening, Margo...felt like a swim?" I try to keep my voice light, she's surprised me again. She giggles.

"Good evening to you too, you don't even sound surprised, do you find naked women in your pool on the regular?" Her confidence is returning, her voice bold. *Wait...naked...*

"Unfortunately no...it's possible my love-life would be more robust if that were the case but, you are, in fact, the first." I wink at her, sitting down on a nearby chair.

"Unfortunately?!" She dips under the water too far and sputters indignantly, splashing water at me as I chuckle before sobering, *here goes nothing.*

"Joking...I assure you Margo, the list of women I would hope to find naked in my pool is a very short list of one, and the planets must be in alignment," I wave a hand at the pool, "because here she swims."

"Oh god that's sweet, and weird, well, *I* made it weird showing up naked in your pool...I got your text by the way. I didn't know what to say, because with you I'm an idiot...so I came up with the genius idea to come skinny-dipping in your pool and I was going to send you a sexy little text to come join me, but the lights startled me and I jumped in," her cheeks are red as she stares at me, "and so...here we are...this is a lot more light than I was figuring on," she trails off with a crooked little smile.

As she talks, she raises out of the water unconsciously, and I see the curves of perfect breasts at the edge of the water. My body reacts and I stand, turning to the house, and turn off all the lights except the ones under the waterfall. The dim light is just enough that I can see her, standing in the same place, watching me.

"Oh...see, that's perfect," her voice is quiet as she begins to swim lazily toward the waterfall. Holding her hand under the spray, she touches the tip of one finger to her tongue and glances at me.

"Salt?" Her voice is curious and I nod, finding my voice.

"Yes, I don't like chemicals." That tiny movement was so delicious, her tongue touching her finger, and I don't want to talk anymore. *This isn't like me at all, but I need to stop thinking and start living.* Pulling my shirt over my head, I toss it on the chair. Pushing shorts and boxers off my hips in one motion, I step out of them.

"Ohhh...yes." I hear the whisper of her sigh from the other end of the pool as I reach a hand down to the edge and lower myself into the water. Swimming slowly over to her, I stop a few feet away. Her face is mostly shadowed, the light of the waterfall glowing behind her. I can see that her eyes are on me, lips parted, and I close the distance.

Margo meets me, her hands sliding up my chest as I run one of my hands up her arm and hold the back of her neck, the other sliding around her waist. Pulling her to me I kiss those full lips, and she kisses me back, hard. Parting her lips, her tongue slides along the seam of mine and I open. She takes her time, each kiss long and slow...a luxury, there's no need to rush.

Her hands slide up around my neck, and I feel her nipples against my chest. Sliding my hand from her waist up her ribs, I pass a thumb over one, earning a gasp. She kisses the corner of my mouth, my jaw, the side of my neck, and I feel her teeth dig in lightly.

With a groan, I pinch her nipple, eliciting another gasp and she nips my neck again. Leaning down, I put both hands under her thighs and lift, setting her up into a natural seat formed by the waterfall rocks. Smooth with constant water flow, it cradles her perfect ass.

Margo stares down at me, hissing her pleasure as I push my shoulders between her knees nipping up the inside of her thigh. I let her feel my breath over her center before kissing the other thigh lightly, drawing it out. She moans softly.

"I want y-…" Her voice chokes off when I bury my face between her thighs. I feel her fingers in my hair, pulling lightly, as she gasps and sighs. I kiss and lick and gently use my teeth to bring her to the brink, feeling her hips start a slow rhythm, her breath fast.

Standing, I kiss my way up her belly, burying my face between her breasts as I wrap my arms around her waist and lift her, pulling her into the water with me. Her legs tighten around my waist as she slides down, and we're face to face. Her eyes are huge as she stares at me for a moment, one arm around my shoulders. Fingertips flicker across my lips, and I gently bite one, eliciting another delicious sigh as she leans closer, her lips finding mine.

As my hands roam her body, my brain registers that the night air has turned decidedly cooler, and her smooth skin is chilled where it is out of the water. Breaking the kiss, I press my forehead to hers.

Shut Up and Kiss Me

Margo

"May I take you to my bed?" Softly, his formal tone rolls over my skin, and it's not the cold that makes me shiver. Miraculously, my lips wait for my brain and I don't laugh or tease. Instead, I look straight into his eyes and let my heart make the leap.

"Yes." In a whisper I decide, for once, not to ruin this moment by over-thinking. *Or over-talking...* He walks us to the side of the pool nearest the house, setting me on the edge before planting his hands and smoothly getting out. Walking to a shelf nearby, he pulls two towels off the rack, handing me one.

Giving my hair a quick squeeze with the towel so my curls don't drip all over my shoulders, I take a moment to look at him as I dry off. When I jokingly called him a silver fox to

167

scandalize Bree, there was really no joke. He's got that thicker muscle through his shoulders and chest that only age brings. I'm sure in his 20s he was leaner and completely drool-worthy, but I prefer this not-so-baby-faced masculinity. Strong and tan, muscles rolling as he dries off and wraps the towel low around his waist. A few beads of water he missed begin a lazy trail down his chest, and I watch them, mesmerized, until they soak into the towel.

He holds out a hand and I wrench my eyes up to his, pausing only briefly to admire a hint of stubble along his jaw. I think he realizes he has an effect on me, his eyes twinkle and he gives me a roguish grin as our fingers link together. Pulling me close, he kisses me softly and leads me into the house, holding my hand.

Through the kitchen and down a long hall, he pauses in a doorway, pulling me up beside him. We've reached his bedroom, and I wait just a beat for nerves to set in…*nope, nothing, I want him bad.* Stepping through the doorway, I turn and pull him toward me. His eyes darken and a rush of heat zings through my belly. *Maybe next time we can take it nice and slow…* I drop my towel.

Stop Thinking So Hard

Williams

*L*eaving Margo asleep in my bed, I make my way to the kitchen and pour myself a drink. Swirling the whiskey in the glass, I take a sip and walk out to the living room. Turning the fireplace to a low flicker and sinking into one of the comfortable chairs nearby, I finally give my thoughts open rein to stampede through my head.

This isn't like me. I don't do casual flings. I don't know what Margo's motivation is, and I don't know what she wants this to be. I don't even know what *I* want this to be...

Margo is full of life, she's bold and determined, and young. Young enough that potentially wanting children of her own is still very much an option. I know I'm jumping way ahead of myself. Nothing that happened tonight, *although the sex was phenomenal,* indicates that she is looking for a long-term relationship, but I can't stop my line of thought.

It's insanity, really, when I force myself to analyze the last week. My feelings for Margo went from something close to actual dislike, to mere annoyance, to confused attraction, to… whatever *this* is…*dare I say it? No. No I do not.*

This is ridiculous. I was weak and spent time with a beautiful woman. She will awaken later and leave my home. We will return to the wedding detail finalization hell that has heretofore defined our relationship, and that will be…that. *Why does that not comfort me…why do I want more?*

Margo has enspelled me. That is all I can determine.

Before my brain is allowed to continue its treacherous musings, I hear a soft step behind me. Margo steps into the circle of light from the fireplace. She's pulled on my shirt, and her hair is delightfully tousled. My heart pings as her bare feet pad across the carpet. She reaches for my glass, taking a sip as she sinks into my lap. Her other arm loops easily around my shoulders, her fingers lightly playing with my hair as she watches the fire.

It feels as natural as breathing to let my arms slide around her waist and press a kiss on her neck. She gives a light hum of pleasure as she takes another drink. We sit without speaking for several comfortable minutes, sharing my whiskey. I'm almost surprised when I break the silence.

"Tell me about yourself, Margo." She glances at me over the rim of the glass, considering, before she hands it to me. I take a sip, waiting.

"There's not much to tell. I'm a bartender, by choice, got a degree in biology and never left my college job, I love it." She laughs lightly, "If I had my way I'd be living someplace hot and sunny, proud owner of a tiny dive bar on the beach." Taking the glass back, she takes a sip, hands the glass back to me and continues.

"Local girl, two brothers and one sister, that would be Bree's mom," she pauses, thinking. "Pretty regular hobbies, I like to read and I bike. I also like to go to the open studios downtown and do ceramics." She giggles, "so…if you ever want to throw on *Unchained Melody* and make a pot together, I'd be down." Recognizing the movie reference, I laugh with her, "it's a date."

Skimming my hand down her leg, I marvel at how smooth her skin is, letting my fingers draw slow circles on her thigh. She hums again, shifting slightly, as she stands up part-way so that she can put a knee on either side of my hips. Sitting back down, she's straddling me and I realize she's wearing nothing under the shirt. Her hands cup my jaw, tilting my face up to hers, and she stares at me for just a moment before pressing her lips to mine.

Warm and sweet, her lips part and my body reacts wildly, hard and insistent under her. Quickly undoing the buttons of her shirt, I push it open, my hands exploring as she kisses me harder, stopping only to breathe. She gasps when my fingers brush over nipples that have hardened, and the next time she pauses for breath I lean down and capture one with my lips, lightly letting her feel my teeth.

Margo lets out a low moan, and I feel a rush of heat everywhere we touch. Her hips start a slow motion, grinding over me, and I'm cursing the layer of clothing between us. She must feel the same, because she leans back, her feet shifting to the floor and stands, watching me as she shrugs off the open shirt and drops it on the floor. The tent in my shorts makes her smile and I lift my hips off the chair, shoving them off and kicking them aside before sinking back down and reaching for her.

Her fingers dance across my palms, and she pins my wrists to the chair arms as she puts her knees to either side of me again, the motion of her hips tantalizing. I want to be inside her, I want to feel her quake around me again. I let her keep my hands pinned down as she moves faster. She angles her hips and sinks down on me as her eyes roll back and slide closed. Her fingers grip my wrists tightly as she holds still for a moment. It's exquisite torture, allowing her to set the pace, and she slowly begins a rhythm, rolling her hips forward and back, our bodies tightly linked.

Perfect tits sway in front of me, and I lean forward enough to lick one, flicking my tongue on the sensitive curve, smiling when she gasps and moves faster. Kissing and nipping, I hold the rest of my body still, letting her ride.

As she speeds up again, her nails dig into my arms and I know she's close. Her rhythm falters and she spasms over me, head thrown back, as I come undone. Pumping my hips up to meet hers, our bodies pound together and I find my own release as she shudders again with a cry.

Stilling, her forehead presses against mine and her hands release my arms, finding my chest as she breathes hard. Sliding my arms around her waist, I pull her in tight, burying my face in her neck and breathing her in.

Gosh

⟨⟩

Margo

He made me breakfast.

I had briefly envisioned waking up early, tossing a kiss on those stern lips and bailing before things got awkward. I should have known better. He was up, apparently long before me, and I wandered out to the kitchen to find pancakes, bacon, and coffee waiting. He was just finishing putting the food on plates, and he picked up one plate, fork and mug and nodded that I should do the same before leading the way out to the table by the pool.

Sitting in friendly silence, we begin eating. The pancakes are surprisingly good, oatmeal and blueberries, sort of granola or something. After a few bites, he takes a drink of coffee and meets my eyes.

"Where do we go from here," he says softly, looking almost shy as the words ripple out. He glances away, embarrassed, and then looks at me again. I'm torn between a teasing comment and a serious answer, but he deserves serious from me.

"I'm not sure," my voice is soft too, as if saying the words louder will make them mean something different. "I enjoyed last night."

"As did I," he rumbles, "very much." His quiet laugh rolls over me like a warm breeze, and my belly responds by clenching at the new memory of how he felt when our bodies moved together. His eyes get serious, and I feel a ping of nerves.

"You perplex me, Margo." His dark eyes slowly meet mine, and I'm practically holding my breath. "I met you and it was like being hit by a train. You're full of life, you practically *vibrate* with it. I think we can agree that I'm not geared correctly to be your sidekick in this wedding planning business-" laughter bursts from my lips at that, and he gives me a quick smile. "What I *do* want is you. I don't want to play games."

"Wowwww…" the word wheezes out of me like the last creak of a dying accordion, and my cheeks flame. His face falls as he watches me gravely, eyes tightening as he prepares to check out of the conversation.

"No!" I squawk in his face. He startles and I mentally shake myself, trying again.

"Sorry! You just caught me off guard by saying the most perfect things. No one has ever told me I vibrate before, that's really sweet. Also your voice…I don't know if you've figured it out, but you talk like a literature professor and your voice makes velvet sound like a cactus and… Gosh…I really like you." I hear myself sigh and mentally slap myself silly. He's going to take it all back now because I'm a raving lunatic.

Except he's smiling, a real smile, all the way across his face. And I'm smiling back, because…gosh. *I can not believe I said gosh out loud. I don't even care.*

Hey Babe

Williams

I've always tried to be direct with women. I don't like conflicts due to miscommunication. I don't like wondering what they are thinking or feeling, I would prefer that they just tell me so that I can react accordingly. Historically, this has not been an effective technique to engage and maintain relationships.

My marriage ended, mainly, because Tanya was no longer satisfied with the level of attention she was receiving from me. Rather than telling me this, she found attention elsewhere. Her argument, not without merit, was that I should have known she needed more and was unhappy.

Fair point. My argument, also valid, was that she should have told me. Tanya did not see the validity of my argument.

She said that would be akin to making her beg for attention. Our discussions spiraled unpleasantly and subsequently, we divorced.

Margo is different. She has always made her feelings known, generally at high volume. When I told her that I want her to be mine, I don't know which of us was the more surprised.

That was almost a week ago. When she left that first morning, via the front door instead of over the pool fence, I expected that we would slow things down, get to know one another. I found myself for the first time nervously wanting a relationship to work.

All of my experiences with Margo up to this point should have told me that our developing relationship would indeed continue full tilt. In less than one week, I have been to the bar where she works, her apartment and the ceramics studio she frequents, *no we did not recreate the pot-throwing scene.*

She calls me Babe. I like it.

She has pummeled me with questions, some sweet, some ridiculous, and I have tried to answer all of them honestly. This is new territory for me, and for the first time, I'm asking questions too. I find myself wondering what her favorite color is, what flowers she likes, what songs she listens to when she's alone. I've never cared before, but with her, I want to know everything.

And every night, she comes to my bed, and I make her sigh and moan and scream. We fall into a tangle and I stroke her beautiful skin. And every night, when I hear her breathing slow with sleep, I whisper, "I love you" just to hear myself admit it out loud.

Last Call

Margo

I'm in fucking-love. I don't even know how it happened. I thought I had a crush. I decided to go for it and have sex with him, get him out of my system. Knowing what a whack-job I usually become at the start of a relationship, it seemed pretty inevitable that I'd drive him away quickly.

He's still here.

I call him Babe.

It just popped out of my mouth one day and stuck. He was walking into Bree's office at the mansion, and I was standing there. I handed him a final tally for the caterer with a 'here Babe' and, that…was that.

It's six days until the wedding, Nick and Bree returned from their travels early this morning, and I'm meeting her tomorrow for final fittings on her dress. I haven't seen her yet, I wonder what she'll think about me dating *Williams*. She's always found him kind of stern and uptight, not at all like the man he is with me.

I haven't slept in my own bed since the night he found me in his pool. I think I will tonight, I don't want to be that girl that just moves in weirdly. I'm working the closing shift at the bar anyway, so it'll be late. As I make final rounds for last call, my mind is on him.

I want this to work. It's hard to wrap my brain around that, I've always been so independent, doing what I please, when I please. Mulling that over, it occurs to me that this is the first relationship I've ever been in where I haven't had to change a thing about myself. I still do what I please, when I please...I just want him to be there with me.

Smiling, I wipe down the bar, humming a tune. Hearing the bells above the entrance jingle, I glance at the clock before turning towards the door.

"Sorry, last call is ov-" I cut off confused, because he's here. He carefully walks across the room and takes a seat on the stool across the bar from where I stand.

"Babe? What are you doing here this late?" Looking closer I think he might be a little drunk. He gives me a cute grin, swaying slightly. Yep, a little.

"I had dinner with Nick, and then we got to reminiscing. I was going to take a cab home, but we were only a couple of blocks away and I decided to take a chance that you were still here." He glances at me with a small smile. "I just wanted to see you." *Melted. Right in a puddle went my heart.*

"Oh Babe, that's sweet, I'm just getting ready to close up, want something to eat?" I raise my voice so that Mandy, the waitress ringing out the final customer can hear me.

"Mandy, can you lock up the front? And then head on home honey, drive careful," she nods, smiling and sketches me a wave as she herds the last folks out the door.

"I got it Margo, have a good night."

Walking around the bar, I link my arm through his, pulling him off the bar stool towards the kitchen.

"Fried eggs and toast, best late night food there is…coming up." As I guide him down a short hall to the kitchen, he takes my hand that's holding his arm, lifting it to his lips. He brushes a kiss across my knuckles.

"That sounds delicious." He says simply, allowing me to lead the way.

Parking him at the old wooden table in the kitchen, I fry us some eggs and butter up several pieces of toast while he watches me quietly. Setting our plates at the table, I settle in across from him and we tuck in. As I'm ungracefully chewing a large bite of toast…I realize he's staring at me.

"You're beautiful Margo." *I'm eating toast and I just worked for nine hours and I'm a train wreck and…oh I love him.*

"You might be drunker than I thought, Babe," I tease, because I never was able to handle a compliment.

"Maybe," he nods sagely, "yet the amount of alcohol imbibed does not add to your beauty, it is difficult to enhance perfection." *Jesus Pete, now that's a compliment.* He nods at me again and then focuses on his food, taking a huge bite. Chewing as he contemplates for a moment, his eyes return to mine.

"I have plans for you and I," his normally silken tones are muffled by food, "If you'll have me, that is." He chuckles at some internal joke, continuing to mow through his plate. I push mine closer and he smoothly transitions to my food. At this point I'm just waiting for the next words to roll out of his mouth. I've never seen him this relaxed, he's usually so careful with his words, thoughtful, I don't want to miss anything.

Sitting back in his chair with a sigh, he looks as if he's about to say something else when his attention is drawn to the counter behind me. He stands abruptly and walks around the table, and as I turn, I see the old radio the cook keeps near the grill. Flipping it on, he fiddles with the dial briefly and an old 80s power ballad fills the room. *80s power ballads are my kryptonite, he can not possibly have known that...*

Turning back, his eyes focus on me in a way that makes the air feel electric, and he holds out his hand.

"I believe you owe me a dance." *This is like the very best part of a movie, right here.* His voice is low and his hand is warm. I stand, he pulls me toward him and our bodies align. He puts our linked hands over his heart and his other arm slides around my waist. I feel his breath in my hair as I rest my cheek on his chest and we move to the music. *Very. Best. Part.*

Sometime later, I pull into his driveway and park, we sleepily walk up to the door and he silently leads me down the hall. Turning, he gently nudges my hands out of the way and undresses me slowly, laying a kiss on my skin as he exposes it, my shoulder, my belly, my hip.

Reaching for the buttons on his shirt, I follow his lead, pushing it off his shoulder, laying kisses on his neck and chest. He gives a tiny shiver at my touch. Encouraged, I go exploring, feathering tiny kisses down his body until his boxers are straining to contain him. His skin is so hot, and he's standing so still, letting me take my time.

Pushing the boxers off his hips I crawl on the bed on hands and knees, looking over my shoulder with a wink. Shaking my ass, I hear him groan and feel the bed dip as he gets behind me. His hands coast over my ass, lightly squeezing, and he pushes into me hard, I gasp as our bodies meet. He holds me tight against him and then pulls out and drives in again.

Feeling his rhythm, I push back to meet him, his fingers dig into my hips and he moves faster and faster, pounding me forward into the bed. Arching my back I lift my hips. The angle sets him right over my g-spot and fingers bunching up the sheets, I scream my pleasure. He keeps pounding, letting me ride out my orgasm until I feel him shudder behind me.

He slows and leans down to kiss my shoulder, wrapping an arm around my waist. Pulling me with him, we end up spooning, his hand tucked in both of mine on my chest. I hear his breathing even out, I'm so relaxed, and right before sleep takes me, I hear him softly murmur.

"I love you."

Surprise seals my lips shut for a moment and as I finally whisper, "I love you too," a light snore escapes his lips.

The Deal Breaker

Williams

Margo is gone when I wake up. Pulling on some clothes I wander out to the kitchen and start some coffee. She's left a note on the counter.

Babe,

Bree's dress fitting is this morning, she wants the four of us to do a late lunch, she was giggling so the cat must be out of the bag. You snore like a freight train when you've been drinking.

Hopefully you weren't talking in your sleep...

I love you too.

I read her words a dozen times, heat blooming in my gut. *Hopefully you weren't talking in your sleep...I love you too.*

In this whirlwind that has become my time with Margo, everything has been perfect. With one exception.

I have a secret.

It might be a deal-breaker.

I need to tell her before we take this any further.

Glancing at the clock, I grab my mug of coffee and head for the shower. I'll tell her tonight, come what may.

Incubator Blues

Margo

"I am a damn genius. It's fine, you can say it." I'm gloating, *but it's true.*

"You are, and it's going to be your fault my make-up is ruined when I turn into one of those happy-crying idiots about my own wedding dress." Bree's voice warbles and she gives a little hiccup, staring into the mirrors.

Bree has always dreamed of having a dress made specially for her, so I found the designer of the dress Bree wore on her first date with Nick. Emerson came through with a vintage lace and silk ball gown that amazed me every time I looked at it on the form. Now, finally seeing it on Bree, it is more than perfect.

The top is ivory silk that fits her to perfection, off her

shoulders with a lace sleeve around her upper arms. Her golden curls will be piled up on her head with a mid length veil on an ornate comb underneath, edged in the same vintage lace.

The skirt is a dream. Barely dusting the floor, layers of tulle hold up ivory silk with a detailed handmade lace overlay. Emerson was able to source more of the raw silk and ribbon in the beautiful scarlet of her first date dress as well as in a deep violet. The scarlet forms a narrow belt and then weaves down into the lace of the skirt, the heavy lace trimming the bottom is a garden of scarlet and violet with tiny hints of emerald green.

Peeking out from under the skirt are the softest, most buttery pale ivory cowboy boots. Bree teared up again when I brought them out and helped her step into them.

"I'm glad you like them Sugarpop, because this is all you get to see until the big day," I grin at her as Emerson and his assistant move in to make final tweaks and pin up the hem.

"If everything is as perfect as this dress and these boots, I suppose I can wait," she smiles, eyes shining, "I love you Margo, you're so good at all this."

"Well, elegant country wedding no holds barred is a pretty fun gig," I lean in for a quick hug and then step back out of the way.

"Can I at least see your dress?" She does that big doe eyed thing, her hands clasped like a little kid.

"Not today, Lovely, you'll just have to wait." Emerson steps back smiling at me, "Margo had her fitting yesterday, yours will be the most beautiful wedding party this city has ever seen." His assistants begin helping Bree out of the dress and when she comes out of the fitting room in her regular clothes, she links arms with me.

"So, I hear this lunch with the boys is more of a double-date?" Bree teases as we walk to her car, "I was surprised when Nick told you bagged the *silver fox*," we both dissolve into giggles like grade-school girls on a playground. I spend the drive to the restaurant filling her in on the details *without too much detail*, our disastrous date at Finleys *and why I call him Babe*, falling into his pool, his whispered 'I love you' when he was drunk. As we settle into a booth at Bellini's, my favorite Italian bistro, to wait for the guys, Bree looks at me earnestly.

"He's older than you by a bit," she's being careful, and I wonder where this is going.

"He is…I'm in my thirties, it doesn't seem to matter much?" Keeping my tone light I take a drink of sangria, watching her over the rim of the glass.

"Oh, no, of course not, I mean he's great and I'm over the moon that you hit it off…" she falters a bit and the rest comes out in a rush, "it's just that Laurel is pretty close to *my* age… does he *want* to have any more kids?"

OH, that's what this is about, the countdown to motherhood.

"Well I certainly hope not, because I'm not his girl if he does." Bree's mouth forms a surprised 'O' at my words, and I laugh. "Seriously? I mean I guess we never talked about it because I haven't dated anyone I saw a future with until now. Can you imagine me with a baby? Like, my own baby? No fucking way. I am going to be the cool-as-shit aunt to all your little rugrats but I have no desire to be a mother." It feels weird to say all that out loud, as if it's wrong not to want children. I've honestly never felt a single tick out of my biological clock. I just can't picture it, I love my freedom, my weird night-owl schedule, everything.

"Okay then…that's not even an issue," Bree recovers from

her initial surprise. "I guess I never asked because I always pictured myself getting married and having a baby, but I'm going to be honest here, I think you as a 'cool-as-shit aunt' is right on the money." She taps her fingers thoughtfully on her glass, smiling, "I'm going to put that on a t-shirt."

"Yeah, it's funny, in my 20s it was harder, your Grandma Jenny was always asking me when I was going to settle down, she always seemed so surprised when I wasn't like my friends. So many of them graduated high school and it was all, 'Oh I can't wait to get married and have babies! It's going to be amazing!'" Taking another drink, I shrug at Bree, smiling.

The conversation moves on, Bree is bubbling with fun stories from her recent travels and plans for the gallery opening. Nick arrives a few minutes later. Giving Bree a kiss he smiles at me.

"Williams isn't here yet? He's usually early." Nick seems to be taking our new relationship in stride, I have no idea what Babe told him about us.

"Yeah, I haven't heard from him, maybe traffic?" My phone pings and I fish it out of my purse.

Babe: I won't make lunch, something has come up.

"Oh well, that's weird, guess I'm third-wheeling it today," Flashing Bree the phone, I'm wondering what 'something' is, so I shoot him back a quick text.

Me: Something? Sounds mysterious, so I'll see you later?

Nick and Bree don't seem concerned, we order and enjoy our lunch. Bree drops me off at my apartment and we say our goodbyes before I hear my phone ping again. Walking in the door, I kick off my shoes with a sigh and flop on the couch, checking the text.

Babe: No. Not tonight. I apologize, I should do this in person. I don't think I'm right for you, we should just be friends until the wedding. I'm sorry.

Sitting up like I was stung by a bee, I read his words again. And then one more time to be sure. *Did he just send me a break-up text? With no explanation at all? What the fuck is this, Junior High?* I call him. Straight to voicemail.

Standing, I have too much nervous energy to burn all of a sudden. I find myself pacing back and forth, trying to understand what could have happened between leaving his bed this morning and lunch. *What. The. Fuck.*

Grabbing my purse and keys, I leave the apartment.

Swing and a Miss

Williams

I couldn't say why I'm back at Finley's, the place where I met my first wife, and then had my first date with Margo. Glutton for punishment I suppose. Setting a beer on the table, I grab a bat and turn on the machine. Falling into a rhythm of *foomp,* swing, *crack, foomp,* swing, *crack,* I hit 20 or so and then step back for a drink. I don't want to think right now. Ending things with Margo was for the best.

"-can't wait to get married and have babies! It's going to be amazing!" Margo's words echo through my mind. I'd arrived at Bellini's early, as is my custom, and as I approached the booth where they were seated, those words burst from her lips and I froze. They couldn't see me. Without another thought, I turned and left.

I can't give Margo the life she wants.

I was going to tell her tonight, but it doesn't matter now. Stepping back up, I turn the machine on again. *Foomp,* swing, *crack, foomp,* swing, *crack.* When my shoulder muscles start to protest and the bottle is empty, I leave. Getting drunk over a woman won't make me feel better.

Leaving the bar, I sit on the bench outside, not sure where I'm going.

My heart aches.

"Fancy meeting you here." Margo's voice is quiet, angry. Burying my feelings deep, I look up at her.

"I realize a text was less than ideal, but there isn't much more to say." I keep my voice as neutral as I am able. She looks so beautiful, standing there, glaring at me.

"Is this because of that stupid note? Did I freak you out?" She stomps over and sits on the bench beside me. "You said it first, *by the way.* I liked it, so I left the note." She huffs out an annoyed sigh.

"I've said it every night you've spent in my bed, this was just the first time you heard it," *I don't know why I told her that, it just makes things worse.*

"Then what the fuck Babe?" Her eyes are shining with unshed tears. *What the fuck indeed.*

Oh... You... Gahhhh

Margo

My heart kicks into high gear. *I want to just climb in his lap and kiss him all over, but I am so confused right now.* He's looking at me and his eyes are so sad, and I'm about to cry angry tears, which just pisses me off even worse.

"I can't give you the life you want, Margo." His voice is low and his gaze drops to his hands.

"What the hell does that mean? How do you know what I want? I have a life, thanks, I just thought maybe we could overlap yours and mine." I'm spitting the words, and I have a feeling I'm missing something important here, but he needs to start making some damn sense.

"Look at me, Babe." His eyes slowly meet mine and I try to calm down. "I thought we had a good thing going, the kind of thing that maybe becomes a forever thing. What in the hell can't you give me that made you walk away?" It didn't work, I'm not calm, and by the end I'm almost yelling.

"Children." He says it so finally, his dark eyes staring into my soul.

"You can't give me children?" *Where the hell did this come from?*

"No."

"Did you get snipped after Laurel or something?" *Snipped? I'm such an asshole. Whatever.*

"No. Laurel is not biologically mine. I was in a car accident as a teenager, there was a lot of internal bleeding, it's not possible for her to be mine." His eyes are pained, this is an old hurt.

"Oh, Babe..." He waves it off, he doesn't want sympathy.

"Tanya strayed, the fault wasn't Laurel's. For years I thought the doctor was wrong and Laurel was a miracle baby. When I found out that the affair that broke us up was not the first... I had Laurel tested. I told her when she was old enough, and offered to assist her in talking to Tanya about her birth father. She declined, I'm her father." The words are clipped, tense.

"And somewhere along the line you made the leap that I need to have babies?"

"I overheard you in the restaurant telling Bree how anxious you are for marriage and a family."

Ohhh, this is making more sense.

"No, you didn't."

"Your words were clear."

"And out of context. You heard me telling Bree how I felt like an oddball when all of my friends got so giddy at the idea of getting married and becoming incubators." *This was dumb. He missed a perfectly good lunch. And scared the crap out of me.*

"What do you mean, Margo?" He's looking confused now, and he deserves it, I narrow my eyes at him.

"I mean, setting aside for a moment options like adoption for people who can't have kids together, I never said I wanted a baby. I don't. I'm planning on winning all the awards in the 'Cool Aunt' category. Don't you *dare* break up with me in a text again."

I Saved This For You

Williams

S ome time later, I've apologized sufficiently for eavesdropping, jumping to conclusions, leaving without speaking to her first, sending a breakup text, and in general 'scaring the crap out of her for no good reason'. Margo and I are once again sitting in the chair before the fire at my home, sharing whiskey after a night swim. Handing me the glass, Margo turns and cups my face in her hands, looking at me seriously for a moment. Leaning in, she kisses me, long and slow.

"I love you," she breathes, giving me another soft kiss.

"And I love you." I kiss her again and then bury my face in her neck, breathing in her warmth, she tastes of whiskey and smells of strawberries. I hug her tightly and then sit back. She looks at me questioningly.

"I have something I would like to show you," she is this important.

"Something good?" She teases amiably, standing to let me up.

"Yes. I am hoping, to steal your phrasing, that it does not cause you to 'freak out'." Standing, I hold out my hand and she laces her fingers through mine. I lead her to my office, waving her toward the couch while I head for a small safe in the closet. Quickly spinning the dial, I open it and pull out a box, approximately the size of my hand. Locking the safe, I join Margo on the couch. Her eyes are bright, full of curiosity.

"Before I show you this, I want to tell you how I came to have it," I hold the box so she can see it, she nods quickly, smiling. "I'm also guessing this will come as no surprise to you, but it's important that you know. I'm not a spontaneous person." A tiny snort of laughter slips out of her and we both smile. "No, it's true. In fact there has been one significant act of complete spontaneity that I can recall in my life. It was the day I bought this." I hand her the box, but lay my hand on it so she doesn't open it yet.

"So the story behind what's in that box starts years ago, when I was young and naive, before I ever met Tanya." Margo's eyes tighten and I kiss her softly before continuing. "Two good things came from my marriage to Tanya. Laurel, and the lesson that what I had with Tanya wasn't love, so I should keep looking." Margo's eyes soften, her fingers light on the back of my hand.

"I bought a ring once. It was just there, perfect, and to my eyes it symbolized the woman I was looking for, the woman that would someday be mine forever." I stop for a moment, ordering my thoughts, this isn't really about Tanya, but she *is* a part of the story. "Tanya and I met and I was in over my head before I knew it." I shake my head, feeling as if I'm clearing the memories of that roller coaster ride of young love.

"Before I had a chance to show Tanya my perfect ring, she hauled me to a jewelry store to show me one she had picked out with her friends. It didn't even occur to her that I wanted to find something special. She picked out a garish show piece, but it made her happy and so it was hers." Lifting my hand off the box, I continue.

"The important thing is, I kept my perfect ring. Maybe some part of me knew even then that what I had with Tanya wasn't real. Maybe I knew that someday I would meet the person worth giving the ring that *I* picked out." Margo's eyes are locked on me.

"When I walked into the antique dealers that day, it was there, sparkling in the case, and it was the most beautiful thing I had ever seen. Just like you." She looks down at the box and opens it slowly. Lifting out the small pouch inside, she loosens the strings with trembling fingers.

"Margo, I promise to love you forever. Will you marry me?" My throat feels tight, my heart is thumping in my chest.

One single tear slides down her cheek. She looks up at me, her lips stretching in a full smile. She nods her head several times before finding her voice.

"Yes, yes, yes!" She whispers, and tilting the pouch over her hand, she lets out a gasp when the ring lands on her palm. The band is thick, the deep almost rose gold color of antique gold rings. A two-carat champagne diamond twinkles in the center, princess cut. To either side sits a one-carat round pale yellow diamond. It glows warmly against her skin. I reach out and take it from her, she carefully holds out her left hand, barely trembling, as more tears slide down her smiling cheeks. It slides on her finger as if it was made for her alone, a perfect fit.

Margo stares at the ring for a few more seconds and then dives into my arms, smothering my face with kisses until we are both breathless and laughing. Curling into my chest, she holds out her hand, flourishing the ring.

"I couldn't imagine anything more perfect," she whispers, "that's all I can say…it's perfect." Every bit of tension leaves me as she utters those words. She's *my* perfect. Tucking her head against my shoulder, she gets quiet, fingers lightly stroking a path up and down my forearm. I can't stop smiling as I watch her eyes follow the ring with the movement of her hand. After a few minutes she lifts her head, and a mischievous look slides across her face.

"You realize Babe, what time it is?" Glancing at a non-existent watch on her wrist she jumps up and feigns a look of horror. "I've got to get started! I've got another wedding to plan!"

Cheers

Margo

The look on his face is priceless. Horror mixed with love, it's a beautiful thing. I can't hold it long before I burst into giggles and his arms wrap around my waist, pulling me back into his lap.

"I'm joking, this wedding for Nick and Bree has been a dream to plan, and it's going to be amazing, but I don't want that kind of attention focused on me. We'll have to think of something smaller...something fun." I let out an involuntary yelp as he slides an arm under my legs, scooping me up with him as he stands.

"I can think of several fun things we should do right now," he growls right in my ear. Carrying me down the hall, he shoulders open the door to his room and tosses me on the bed.

Pulling his t-shirt smoothly over his head, he shoves his pants and boxers off his hips and kicks out of them as he reaches for me. Grabbing my hips, he pulls me closer. I'm only wearing a thong and one of his t-shirts after our swim and he shoves the shirt up around my ribs. Glancing at my thong he lets out a low growl and snaps the lace like it's paper, letting it flutter to the floor. *Damn, I liked that thong...oh welllllohmygod.*

Every thought is driven straight out of my head as he pushes my legs over his shoulders and buries his face between my thighs. The prickle of his jaw and the heat of his breath and *ohmygod* his tongue sets my back in an arch that would be painful if he wasn't making me feel so damn good. My toes *literally* curling, it's only a few exquisite minutes and I'm screaming my pleasure, nails scrambling for his hands that are tight on my hips, holding me still for him.

Kissing his way up my belly, he buries himself in one thrust, letting out a groan as his eyes slide shut and he holds still for a moment. Pulling out he drives in again, holding his weight up off me, I stare down my body as he moves. *That is the hottest thing I've ever seen.* Pistoning his hips several more times, he pulls away from me and gets off the bed.

Grabbing my hips, he pulls me to the edge of the bed and wraps my legs around his neck, driving in deep again. Pounding hard, his dark eyes sear into mine. Turning his head slightly, he licks the inside of my calf and then bites it, setting his teeth just enough that I lose myself and I'm over the edge, delicious spasms rippling through my core. I feel him change his angle, his strokes shortening, and I move my hips with him, hard and fast until he loses his rhythm. Burying himself deep one more time, he falls off his own cliff with a groan.

Letting my legs fall around his waist, he lifts one, watching me, and lightly bites my ankle one more time with a smile. I gasp and shiver as an aftershock rolls through me. Letting my feet slide past his hips to the floor, I stand as he backs away and walks to the huge bath, turning on the taps.

Sinking into the hot, sudsy water, I let out an audible moan and he smiles. He pads out of the room naked. I admire the view and then slide down in the water until the bubbles tickle my chin. Returning a few moments later, he sets two glasses on a table near the tub as well as an ice bucket holding a bottle of champagne. Pulling the champagne out of the ice, he pops the cork and fills our glasses, stepping into the tub and sinking down into the water facing me.

"To forever," he murmurs, lifting his glass towards mine.

"I'll drink to forever," I clink my glass lightly on the edge of his and drink.

Moon and Stars

Williams

The day of Bree and Nick's wedding dawns with the promise of blue skies and sunshine. Margo meets Bree for brunch and then the seemingly onerous process of 'getting ready' begins. Margo's ring is safely tucked away with me, she didn't want to weather the barrage of questions from family that will be present at the wedding, it would detract from Bree's moment.

I have been sent to locate Nick, keep him calm and happy, and make sure he arrives at the estate at the appropriate time, no sooner, certainly no later. There are to be pictures prior to the ceremony while the sun is still shining. The ceremony itself is to take place at sunset.

Nick and Bree's story involves an heirloom black diamond

ring, and the advice his father once gave him to 'find his night'. Nick's father said that he would know he'd found love when he wanted to spend not only his days with her, but every last one of his nights. When Bree shared the story of Nick's parents, Margo fell in love with the entire idea of a night wedding.

Keeping Nick calm and happy will not be a chore. I pick him up at the hotel Margo sent them to in order to keep them out of the way and the wedding decorations a surprise. Nick has become good friends with one of Bree's brothers, Andrew. He rounds out the wedding party, arriving at my home shortly after we return. Anthony and Nathan, Bree's other brothers accompany him, they will usher Bree's mother and grandmother in before the ceremony.

We have time for coffee by the pool and then the men's version of a beauty squad invades. We all endure their ministrations with good-natured embarrassment.

Arriving at the estate, Margo's team immediately diverts us to a dressing area. Once Nick is ready, one of the staff Margo has on hand escorts him to the mansion. With photos being taken prior to the ceremony, Margo wanted to give Nick and Bree a moment in private. While they are in the mansion, Margo and Bree's sister Clary arrive and we walk a short distance to the carriage house and gallery where the wedding will take place.

Margo is a vision. I could not be more entranced by her beauty if it were her wearing the white dress this day. It is difficult not to stare at her as we get some of the initial wedding party pictures completed, and a horde (nine, to be fair) of small children are ushered in, all dressed in sparkling silver and pale grey. Children of Bree's many cousins, they are an adorable, laughing bundle of energy.

The little girls have flower crowns of roses and deep purple orchids with ribbons in scarlet, violet and a dark emerald green streaming down the backs. Their skirts are like tutus magnified. Clouds of silver tulle float around them as they bounce and run and laugh. The boys are in dove grey pants and white button downs, untucked, with the smallest of boutonnieres worn proudly on their chests.

Andrew and Clary are wearing shades of grey that are darker than those on the children. Margo and I are in a deeper shade yet. Clary and Margo are wearing dresses that have a fitted silk top, off the shoulder with lace forming a sleeve around the top of their arms. The full skirt flares out in what I would call (and Margo would surely correct) a 50s style. Layers of tulle with an intricate lace over the top, they stop at just above ankle length and silvery grey cowboy boots peek out when they move. The boots themselves are works of art, soft, supple leather, hand-stitched with flowers to mimic the colors on the little girls flower crowns.

The men are wearing suits in corresponding shades of grey, Nick is in a deep charcoal. All of us have boots to wear as well, black with minimal stitching. The gradation from the silver of the children to the dark, rich grays is amazingly effective, I can imagine how wonderfully this will all photograph. As I observe the wedding party, taking in the details, I catch Margo's eye. She raises one eyebrow at me, and I walk over to her side.

"Every color, stitch, flower and fabric is a stroke of genius," I gently kiss her temple, "I should have left you alone to work your wedding magic from the start." Margo lets out a 'hmmph' followed by a delicate snort.

"Babe, wedding planning is my *jam*," she punctuates this with a fist pump, and we both dissolve into helpless laughter. We turn at the sound of the flower girls squealing.

"You look like a princess! Do you have a crown? Can I touch your dress?" Their little voices rise in excitement as Bree and Nick enter the room, arm in arm. Nick's face is happily stunned, and he keeps looking at Bree as if he can't believe she is real.

Bree is radiant. Her dress is a confection of lace and tulle and ribbons that indeed transforms her into a boot-wearing princess. Her golden hair is piled in an intricate configuration on her head, a classic antique comb holds the veil in place at the back. Black diamonds sparkle in her ears, mirroring the one on her right hand. Her left hand is bare, ready for the band tucked in a small velvet box in my pocket.

Margo is poetry in motion as she herds everyone to the area where the ceremony will take place. The photographer takes over, and the first wave of photos begins. As I dutifully line up as directed, I'm looking around at the magic that has been spun in this space. The gallery is a huge open area with a mixture of contemporary, clean white interspersed with polished barn wood. Dozens of antique lanterns are strategically hung from the rafters, low over the crowd in a twinkling mobile. High up in the rafters roughly one million tiny twinkle lights emit a golden glow.

At one end of the gallery, a huge barn wood doorway has been transformed into the area where Nick and Bree will exchange vows. A breathtaking garland of orchids, roses, and a host of flowers I can't begin to identify festoons the arch, all in deep pink, scarlet, and violet with deep emerald greenery. All along the side walls of the main gallery, heavy wooden plant stands of varying heights have been strategically placed, each with a large bouquet to mimic the garland. The scent is incredible, the rich perfume of the flowers lingering pleasantly in the fresh country air.

As the men are sent off to the side so that the photographers can take pictures of Bree with her bridesmaids, the artistry of the color choices becomes clear. Ranging from deep charcoal to the silver on the children, Bree stands out like a new moon at dusk with the children serving as shimmering stars.

Hitched Without A Hitch

Margo

The wedding party pictures complete for now, the guests are being ushered to their seats. Family pictures will take place after the ceremony while the guests are ushered to the carriage house for drinks. Everything is flowing smoothly and according to schedule. *I'm just annoyed that I didn't factor in a fifteen minute interval someplace private with Babe because, daaaammmnnn can that man fill out a suit.*

The string quartet in the balcony of the gallery begins playing and the guests fall silent as Susan and Grandma Jenny are escorted in and seated at the front. Nick steps out of the side chamber near the archway and stands, waiting for his bride. *Showtime.*

Clary and Andrew step out right on cue as the music changes

again and march slowly up the aisle. Giving Bree one last look, she's standing with her father, they're chatting softly, she's calm and happy. Feeling my eyes, she glances my way and gives me a quick wink.

I turn to find Babe, standing close, arm held out for me, smiling. Taking his elbow, we step out and march down the aisle, and my eyes might be just a little misty. Before we part, he lifts my hand to his lips and whispers, "I love you".

As we take our spots and turn to watch, the flower girl and ring bearer herd draws a large sigh and several laughs as the crowd falls victim to the cuteness overload. They bounce, walk, run, crawl *and in one precocious case, somersault,* down the aisle in a flurry of giggles.

After a pause, the music changes once more, and Bree and her father appear. The collective gasps, oohs and aahs are music to my ears. *Nailed it.* Bill is trying hard to be stoic, but his eyes are suspiciously shiny. He kisses Bree and then places her hand in Nick's with a quiet word that makes Nick smile and nod.

The ceremony begins, and my mind races forward to the rest of the evening. So much planning has gone into this wedding, every detail perfect. My attention snaps back to the business at hand as Nick and Bree begin to exchange vows. They wrote them and kept them secret, *even from me, eye roll,* until this moment. Bree's clear voice doesn't waver as she speaks.

"Nick, I promise to love you for the rest of my life. I can't think of anything else I can promise that is more important. I also promise to hog the blankets, wreak havoc in the kitchen and make you sit through every one of my favorite 80s movies…twice." She pauses as the crowd chuckles appreciatively. "You are mine and I am yours, and that will always come first. If I am your night, you are my morning. Every day that dawns with you I will be thankful for, forever." She finishes simply and smiles as she looks into Nick's eyes. More than one guest is reaching for a tissue, Susan is sobbing happily as Bill wraps an arm around her shoulders. Nick clears his throat lightly and begins.

"Bree, I knew you would be able to find the words, and the temptation was great to write, 'ditto' as my vow." He pauses, glancing over her shoulder at me, a twinkle in his eye, "Knowing that Margo would quickly find an untraceable way to kill me after all the work she's done," he pauses to wait for the chuckles to die down, *hardy har har.* "I decided to attempt to put into words what you mean to me." He reaches out a hand, and she takes it in both of hers.

"A life with you feels like more than any man deserves," his voice is low, but clears as he continues. "A life with you will be full of love, laughter and joy. I look forward to every single day we have together, every smile I put on your lips, every sparkle in your eye. I promise to take care of you, caffeinate you, warm your toes, and kiss you goodnight. And I promise to spend the rest of my life loving you."

There is not a dry eye in this place. *Those were the mic drop of all vows. Wow.*

The Most Perfect Thing

Williams

As I hand Nick the ring to place on Bree's finger, a row of black diamonds on a delicate gold band, my heart surges with happiness for him. They are pronounced man and wife, and Nick tilts Bree into a deep dip as they kiss, to squeals of delight from the children.

My mind is on Margo, and the pictures and the toasts are over without delay. Nick and Bree share the first dance and Margo is finally able to put away her tablet. Finding her in a small side room, I walk up behind her and slide my arms around her waist, kissing the back of her neck. She leans back into me with a contented sigh.

"Babe, this was a perfect wedding…but not for me, so much planning, wow…" she giggles, "maybe we should just run away together." She turns in my arm and tilts her face up for a kiss.

"It's interesting the way our minds occasionally align, my love." I'm nervous now, but if she was serious…

"Align? The look on your face is making me nervous, what's going on?" Her beautiful eyes scan the area as if an answer will appear.

"Will you marry me, Margo?"

"Yes, of course, I thought that was the plan?" She's amused now, playful.

"Will you marry me right now?" Taking her hand, I lead her outside, back to the now-empty gallery. Empty except for the minister. Margo sees him and then stares at me for a moment.

"Right now? Ohmygod, sorry," she glances at the minister who smiles gently.

"Babe? Do you mean this?"

"Nothing would give me greater joy than becoming your husband today, Margo." It's true. She's mine, I'm hers, the end.

"Oh…you always say the most perfect things," she sighs happily.

You've Got Mail

Three Weeks Later

Bree

Nick brings in the morning mail, flipping idly through the stack as he leans on the kitchen counter. I'm at the stove, flipping the last pancake onto a plate. He sets most of the pile on the table and then mutters as he scans a bright yellow envelope more closely.

"What's that?" I hand him a mug of coffee and head back to the counter for our plates. Joining me at the table, he holds out the envelope with a smile.

"It's from Margo," he laughs as I practically rip it out of his hand. It's the first I've heard from her beyond a cryptic 'I'll be in touch' text late on our wedding night.

The card inside has one of those cats with great big eyes that looks like it's begging for bacon on the cover. Shaking my head,

I open it with a smile. The inside says, 'Happy Birthday', but the words have been crossed out and replaced with, 'Sorry, Babe bought this card, I told him to get something cute, I should have been more specific'. A folded paper rests inside, I unfold it and find Margo's familiar handwriting.

* * *

Sugarpop,

I hope this card finds you and Mr. Perfect happy as clams with your new life together. The sweetness overload was making me sick so I had to bail.

JUST KIDDING, I love you, and I'm so happy for you, and now I want to tell you not to worry about me, I got my own happily ever after. That said, it is currently a wifi-free happily ever after. I'm workin' on it, but it's snail mail for now.

Babe and I poached your minister and got married. Side note: I can't wait to show you my ring it's a-fucking-mazing.

The surprises don't stop there though, you're going to need to make a trip to the Caribbean sometime soon, tiny island called St Lamoix, find the main street and ask someone to point you to Margo's Place.

XOXO,
  Margo

* * *

Read on for a taste of the next story...it's Veronica's, and it's not what you're expecting.

Finding My One

Rude Awakening

Strong hands cup my jaw, tilting my face up as his lips claim mine. Grazing my lower lip with his teeth he sucks it in to bite it lightly as his hands slide into my hair. Gathering up a handful, he kisses his way along my jaw and pulls my head back, just rough enough that I gasp and then sigh with pleasure.

His other hand slides down my arm to my waist, finds the hem of my shirt and lifts it up, tickling my belly as his hot fingers find my skin. Releasing my hair he uses both hands to push my shirt up, but before I can raise my arms to help, he flips it over my head and then uses one hand to pull it tight at my back, pinning my arms.

I'm panting with need, tits about to burst from the lacy bra that's now on full display. Eyes drinking me in, he palms one, thumb teasing the nipple that's about to drill a hole in the bra. Sliding his hand up to the strap, he slides first one, then other off my shoulders, never letting up the pressure that has my arms pinned to my sides.

Sitting down on the couch, he pulls me closer, his face nuzzling between my tits as one hand slides under my skirt, cupping my ass. I moan *BEEP* and sigh. *BEEP*. His *BEEP* mouth is *BEEP* hot and *BEEP* wet and *BEEP* I struggle *BEEP* wanting to *BEEP*. SON-OF-A-FUCKING-ALARM! DAMNIT! *I can't even get laid in my sleep...doesn't matter, this is not a dry spell, this is a CHOICE. Why would I need a man? I'm rich, I'm young, I'm beautiful, I am having the time of my life.* My tingling clit is not fooled...it would very much like a man to take care of it right now.

Grumbling I fumble for my phone and dismiss the alarm, hoping if I shut my eyes fast enough, my dream man will be waiting. No such fucking luck. With a sigh I sit up, toss my sleeping mask off and get out of bed. Crossing the room I throw open the heavy curtains to let the morning sun wake me up completely.

Stretching I head into the studio adjoining my bedroom, tuning into a podcast to catch up with last night's gossip as I flow through my yoga poses. An hour later I'm feeling centered as I shower and ring for breakfast to be brought to my suite. I have no desire to eat with my father this morning. I'll deal with *him* later.

Pause for Effect

Veronica

"I do not care! Kidney stones? That's horrifying, why would you share that information with me, I don't need to hear that!" I grab the edge of the desk, leaning closer, making sure my point is clear. "Do you know what I *do* need to hear? I need to hear who was in charge of my security detail when I missed Claire Saint James' Red Party. It happened *yesterday* and I missed it because my guard had *kidney stones* and *shockingly* there was no alternate!"

I pause to let the full effect of my astonishment and dismay sink in, no tantrum works if you don't pause for effect. My father is sitting at his desk, not looking at me, I follow his line of sight and glance over my shoulder. The drinks cabinet... figures. He always has looked for a way to hide from his problems. I challenge him at every turn and not once has he ever just stood up to me. I plan to keep pushing until he does, it's my favorite game.

"Tell me, *Father*, how exactly does that happen? How exactly do I have *one security guard*? Why is there not a fucking platoon of them waiting their turn to protect me? YOU are the one who insists that I have these fucking babysitters. Do you understand that just because he had to leave, to go to the damn hospital, my driver refused to take me and wouldn't let me go with anyone else without my guard?!"

Pausing again, mostly because I need to breathe, I open my mouth, preparing to launch into another diatribe.

"Enough." At the sound of her voice, my blood runs ice cold and I swing around, goosebumps speckling my skin.

"Mother," I can't keep the surprise and a tinge of fear out of that one word. "What are you doing here?"

Tough Love Sucks

Veronica

Stiletto heels clicking on the polished wood, Evelyn Rockford strides across the study and pours brandy into two tumblers. Crossing the room, she hands one to my father with a small smile, and then turns to me, leaning back to sit on the edge of his desk. She takes a sip of the brandy, looking at me carefully over the rim of the glass.

Her hair is dark, glossy brown like mine, she has a shot of silver right at the part of hers, and it's rolled up in a twist, not a hair out of place. Dove grey suit with a pencil skirt, white blouse, all tailored to fit her slim body perfectly. Pearls at her neck and ears. The picture of steely success. I come by my ice princess persona through genetics, *and it works on everyone but the woman who gave it to me.*

Silent in this mini battle of wills, I maintain eye contact, pulling the fragments of my cool back around me and settling my nerves. I get what I want, when I want in this world. I raise my chin, carefully keeping my hands in place, refusing to be nervous. *I wish I believed my own bullshit, god I need to pee.*

"I scheduled a break in the lecture circuit to come home," Evelyn says coolly, setting the glass on the desk with a clink and crossing her arms, "because your father and I want to make some changes." We continue our stare-down as my mind races, I don't want anything to change, I like things just the way they are, *my way.*

"You're spoiled Veronica. You always have been and, I know, it's our own monster we've created," she holds up a hand to stop me as my mouth drops open in outrage, *monster?!* "We've always wanted the best for you, and we know that we've been very busy...perhaps too busy to notice that you've become an adult with no appreciation for anything." *Well this is bad, where is she going with this?*

"Why didn't you have a backup guard last night you ask? Because they refuse the job! It's not as if you're in any actual danger of attack, they are mainly there to protect you from making a *fool* of yourself, and the last three companies we've engaged have given back our retainer fee. Most recently because, and I quote, 'that spoiled brat needs a spanking not a babysitter'!" Smoothing her skirt with her hands as she regains control, Evelyn avoids my eyes. Reaching for her glass, my mother takes another sip and then swirls the brandy, her eyes on it, contemplating her next words.

"The Oceanics line is going over like a dream," Evelyn says brightly, "and the market is screaming for more organics. We want to introduce a line of cottons that supplement all the skin care and makeup products, and I'm bringing you in at ground zero." She pauses and glances at me, and I'm thrown off. I don't know what to say, I can't even decide if this is good or bad news.

My parents were born into money, and when they got married, they built an empire of skin care products used exclusively in high end day spas that cater to cruise ship clientele. My mother is the spokeswoman for the brand, she was a model for a haute couture fashion house in Paris when she met my father. He was in a position to get her face time with key players at a time when cosmetic regenerations cruises were the next greatest binge of the wealthy.

Even now, in her late 50s, Evelyn could easily pass for a woman in her 30s. She has perfect skin, rigorously protected from the sun, and she is her own best client of the line that my father's partners developed. Over the years, they've expanded, and cornered the market in organics, another favorite buzzword of the spa set. *Let's only put this shit on our faces if it came from nature with a 600% markup, people are fucking sheep.* My mother is currently on a lecture circuit, bringing new physicians and aestheticians on board, expanding the line.

My sole job since attending university; where I was queen of my sorority and managed to secure a degree in marketing, *in spite of myself and the little weed habit I tried out along the way;* was to be a socialite, maintain my social media presence, and spend Daddy's money. I carefully developed this job for myself, having vigorously resisted my father's early attempts to bring me into the business.

My mother had always been good about leaving me alone, I would occasionally attend seminars with the uber-important clients, assisting mostly by allowing my mother to claim my skin was the result of her Oceanics line. *Joke's on them, I almost never remember to use it, I sleep in my makeup, I just have great skin.* I give her Oceanics line a plug and a hashtag once in a while, and we all live happily ever after. *I thought.*

"I think you'll have to define, 'ground zero' before I decide if I'm interested, Mother." I'm careful to keep my tone cool and respectful, a tiny bit of suspicion coloring my words.

"I think *you'll* have to decide if you enjoy having money or not Veronica," Evelyn counters quickly, voice rising slightly, "you are 29 years old. We are no longer interested in footing the bill for an aging socialite who refuses to use her brains and talent for anything other than spending money she didn't earn!"

AGING? My brain short circuits and I gasp, a hand flying to my mouth in outrage.

"We want you to be happy, darling," my father says quietly. *Well that's fucking hilarious, you want me to be happy? Don't tell me I'm aging at 29.*

"Your father and I just see you going through the motions, attending parties, spending money, but where are your friends? Where is the experience? What memories will you have when you truly are old and grey?" My mother smiles, looking straight into my soul, her blue eyes going stormy grey with emotion.

"We love you darling, and after that little fiasco with Nick," *ugh, do not mention Nick, that one hurt, he was the first man who wasn't just taking me on a test drive because I'm rich and gorgeous, he was good...and we didn't work because of me.* "We just don't want you to become sad and irrelevant," she murmurs, unaware that she has just surgically removed my heart, set it on my father's desk, and lit it on fire.

My eyes narrowing, I spear her with a glance, sharing it with my father who is now watching me instead of his glass of booze. I have no words, my parents are assholes. Turning on my heel, I storm out of the study, catching the door and shoving it shut behind me with a resounding boom. I hear my parent's voices before the door slams but I ignore them, moving quickly up the grand staircase and down a long hall to my wing of the house. Shutting the doors to my suite, I sit at my makeup table, breathing heavily as I stare at my reflection in the mirror.

'Sad and irrelevant'? Well I don't look happy, I'll give them that. My dark brown eyes are glittering with anger and unshed tears. What my mother doesn't understand is that she just casually threw out my greatest fears. I know I haven't done anything with my life. I don't know what I *want* to do, I *hate* being alone.

Although if I'm honest I know it's my own fault. After a few attempts to make friends in high school and college, only to realize that they were looking straight at my trust fund, I stopped trying. Shallow relationships with people who have as much money as I do is all I've been able to manage lately, drinks, parties, shopping, the occasional fling. *My mother is right, I fucking hate it when she's right.*

Leaving all the insulting old-maid commentary out, I think back about the conversation in the study. I'm intrigued by a cotton organics line, and I find myself wondering what she meant by 'ground zero'. But I'll be damned if I'm going to go ask now, no way, not showing this weak underbelly to the shark that is my mother. It can wait until dinner.

When my mother is home, dinner is a formal affair. We eat in the dining room, there are courses involved, and we dress for dinner. I decide to put my best face forward, I refuse to show hurt feelings when I've decided I want to hear what she has to say. I pull a silk sheath in royal blue out of my closet and get ready for dinner as if I'm preparing for battle.

Read Finding My One to find out how a spoiled city girl finds love, and the life she didn't know she needed, in a steamy, small-town, opposites-attract romantic comedy.

* * *

About the Author

Halo Roberts is a writer of steamy rom-coms, lover of coffee and dark beer, and spoiler of two fat cats affectionately known as the Bitchy Betas. She's living happily ever after in Iowa with her very own hunky farm boy, and a small herd of stubborn mules that look a lot like children.

Head on over to haloroberts.com, sign up for Halo's newsletter and receive a free download of her short story, A Night at the Diner.

You can connect with me on:
- http://haloroberts.com
- https://twitter.com/RobertsHalo
- https://www.facebook.com/halorobertsauthor
- https://www.bookbub.com/profile/halo-roberts
- https://www.instagram.com/halorobertswrites
- http://bit.ly/halogoodreads

Subscribe to my newsletter:

✉ http://haloroberts.com

Also by Halo Roberts

Sweet, steamy, laugh-out-loud romantic comedies that always end in a happily ever after…or two.

Finding My Night
Second star to the right…

A sassy chef with a crush on her boss finds herself on a 'not-a-date' with him in this hilariously steamy romp. Complete with a problematic socialite, a cream puff fiasco, and a killer dress with a strategic peek of lace, there might also be a man-bun…a pair of dueling best friends…and a wedding…or two.

Finding My One
Blue skies and dirt roads and peaches, oh my...

A real job with the family business or goodbye trust fund...my parents have lost their minds. The icing on this craptastic cake is setting up headquarters in some backwater southern town, complete with a partner...a rugged, country, single dad that flips every switch I've got...and a few I didn't know about.
~Veronica

Things are heating up in the country...

Finding My Safe
The songs say love is in the water... and strange...

When chance brings Wren and Kane together again, things have changed. Wren is graduating med school, soon to start her residency. Kane is a bouncer at a crappy roadside bar. When an ambush in an alley makes him depend on Wren far more than he expected, can they find love in the midst of five-dollar tequila shots, surprise proposals and the bright lights of Las Vegas?

Here's hoping love is also at Joe's bar...and not actually strange.

Finding My Sun

Breakups suck.

They suck even more after you drunkenly tell your A-list rock star boyfriend that you love him…then find your now ex best friend in his bed. Welcome to Laurel's world. So, what's a girl with a mangled heart to do? Escape to the Caribbean for some sun, sangria, and…a surfer?

Laurel meets Trey and sparks fly, hammocks flip, and all signs point to love. But when best friend and rock star drama invades the island, can new love last? Laurel has decisions to make, hearts to break and a sunburn to avoid in this two-part romantic comedy.